When Bad Meets Bad . . .

"What do you say, gringo?" Rodrigo asked. "Are you as bad as Rodrigo?"

"Probably," Chance said. "What do you think, Cord?"

"Probably badder," Rydell said.

"Then we shall prove it," Rodrigo said. "We will fight for Belinda."

"Fight for a woman?" Chance asked. "There are lots of women, Rodrigo. Go and find another one."

"I am afraid, señor, that I want this one."

"Well, amigo, I've got this one," Chance said.

"So we will fight," Rodrigo said, "with knives. The best man gets the girl, eh?"

Chance looked at Rydell, wh̶

"Okay," Chance said̶ He finally released the girl, wh̶ d up from the table.

Rodrigo ̶ of their sheaths.

"I think yo̶ ance said, "but I'll use my gun."

THE GUNSMITH

387

MEXICO MAYHEM

J. R. ROBERTS

JOVE BOOKS, NEW YORK

THE BERKLEY PUBLISHING GROUP
Published by the Penguin Group
Penguin Group (USA) LLC
375 Hudson Street, New York, New York 10014

USA • Canada • UK • Ireland • Australia • New Zealand • India • South Africa • China

penguin.com.

A Penguin Random House Company

MEXICO MAYHEM

A Jove Book / published by arrangement with the author

For information, address: The Berkley Publishing Group,
a division of Penguin Group (USA) LLC,
375 Hudson Street, New York, New York 10014.

ISBN: 978-0-515-15444-3

PUBLISHING HISTORY
Jove mass-market edition / March 2014

PRINTED IN THE UNITED STATES OF AMERICA

10 9 8 7 6 5 4 3 2 1

Cover illustration by Sergio Giovine.

ONE

The Gunsmith was mired in a state of depression.

He hadn't felt this way since he took refuge in a bottle following the death of his friend Wild Bill Hickok. He had a drink in front of him this time, but there was no danger of repeating the process. He had at least learned that much about himself.

But he was depressed.

Over the past few months, several attempts had been made on his life. In itself, not unusual. The past attempts on his life were countless. But they'd been attempts on his reputation, not his life. These recent attempts, they were personal. Someone had sent the killers against him—*him*, not the Gunsmith. Clint Adams, personally. He had done something to this person to make them want him dead. And there was no way to tell when that was, how long this person had been waiting for their revenge.

Clint had decided to take himself away from it all for a while, had not only ridden to Mexico but had gone all the way to the seaside town of Laguna Niguel.

He got himself a room in a small hotel, spent most of his days sitting in the cantina, nursing beers and eating tacos and enchiladas. His nights were spent with a waitress named

Carmen, who, in her thirties, was the oldest of the three waitresses who worked there. She had a wild mane of black hair, large breasts prominently displayed in peasant blouses each day, and a lust for sex he found pleasantly exhausting.

He had been there two weeks, and was not looking to leave anytime soon . . .

Cord Rydell took off his hat and wiped his sweating brow on the sleeve of his blue shirt, leaving a dark stain.

Next to him his partner, Hal Chance, was similarly wiping his face, but with his wadded-up bandanna. He wiped the inside of his hat and replaced it on his shaggy head.

"This heat is killin' me," he complained.

"The sea air will help," Rydell told him.

"I ain't never seen the sea."

"This will be the Pacific," Rydell said. "It goes on forever."

"Like the desert?"

"Yes, like the desert," Rydell said, "only wetter."

"It's damn hot," Chance complained. "Is it always so hot in Mexico?"

"Well," Rydell said, tiring of his partner's complaints, "it is summer."

"Hot," Chance said, wiping his face again. He grabbed his canteen and took a swig.

"Take it easy," Rydell said, "we don't know when we'll find more water."

"I thought you said you knew Mexico like the back of your hand."

"Yeah, well, I ain't been down here in a while," Rydell said. "Waterholes I thought were there might be dry, so just . . . take it easy."

"Yeah, okay."

"Come on," Rydell said, "we'll stop in the next town and get something to eat."

"And some cold beer!" Chance said.

Finally, Rydell thought, something he could agree with Chance about.

They rode into the town of El Diablo later that day and Hal Chance sniffed the air.

"What's that smell?" he asked his partner.

"That's the ocean," Rydell replied.

"Where is it?" Chance asked, standing in his stirrups.

"Still pretty far away, but close enough to smell," Rydell told him. "Let's stop at that cantina."

"Ya don't have to tell me twice," Chance said.

They reined in their horses in front of a small cantina. As they dismounted, they could smell the food cooking inside. Both their stomachs began to growl. They tied off their horses and went inside. There was a small crudely constructed bar and about eight tables with mismatched chairs. Two of the tables were occupied, and there were three men standing at the bar. All eyes turned to them as they entered, including the two girls lounging at the far end of the bar, waiting for something to do.

"We don't want any trouble," Rydell said as Chance eyed the two Mexican women.

"I never been to Mexico before," Chance said, "but I would love me some Mexican women."

"Well, we ain't here for no Mexican ass, Hal," Rydell said. "We're gonna have a beer, and some food, and get outta here. Got it?"

"I got it, Cord, I got it," Chance said.

"Can we get somethin' to eat?" Rydell asked the bartender.

"*Sí, señor*," the man said, "*siéntese.*"

"What did he say?" Chance asked.

"He said we should sit," Rydell said.

One of the girls leaning on the bar stood up and walked

over to them. She slouched, was a bit chunky, but Chance still eyed her body as she said, *"Que pasa, señores?"*

"Enchiladas," Rydell said, *"y cerveza."*

"Sí, señor. Y frijoles?"

"Sí," he said.

"Inmediatamente."

"What'd she say? Whatta we gettin'?"

"Food's comin' right away," Rydell said. "Just sit back and eat it, Hal."

As the girl went into the kitchen to get their food, the bartender came over with their beers. Chance was eyeing the other girl, still standing at the bar. She was younger, stood straighter, with small tits and a slim waist. Her nipples poked at her peasant blouse as she preened for him and smiled.

The bartender said something in rapid Spanish to Rydell, who answered him, also in Spanish, although not as rapid. The man shrugged and went back to the bar.

"What'd he say?"

"He wanted to know if we wanted the girls."

"What'd you say?"

"I told him we're here for food and drink and that's all."

"Look at that gal, though, Cord!" Chance said. "Look at them little pokies."

"Not now, Hal," Rydell said. "We have no time for that."

"Why not?" Chance asked, "If the guy is loungin' around down here, where's he gonna go?"

"Never mind where he's gonna go, we gotta find out where he is. We got a job to do."

"I know, I know," Chance said, "but that don't mean we can't—"

"Yeah, Hal," Rydell said, "it does mean we can't. Drink your beer."

Rydell drank down half the beer, which was lukewarm, but did cut the dust he'd been swallowing for miles.

Hal Chance drank his, but continued to eye the young girl at the bar, who also continued to give him hot looks.

Rydell knew that Chance was going to cause them trouble. He just hoped they'd be able to eat first before they were forced to kill some of the locals.

TWO

Clint walked along the beach until he came to the house that was built up on stilts.

"Avery!" he called.

After a moment a man came out onto the porch and smiled down at him.

"Come on up!"

Clint walked around to the other side of the house and used the ladder to climb up to the porch. Avery Castle was there waiting for him. If he'd been an uninvited guest, the man would have been waiting with a gun. Instead, he was waiting there with his hand out for a handshake.

"Good mornin'," Avery said. "Welcome. Coffee?"

"Definitely."

"Have you had breakfast?"

"Well, I did, but that was very early," Clint said. "I was kind of hoping I'd be invited."

Avery slapped him on the back and said, "You're always invited, my friend. We eat breakfast late here. Come inside."

Avery, although in his sixties, was barrel-chested and healthy, and the slap on the back almost took Clint's breath away.

"Estralita!" he yelled as they entered. "We got company for breakfast."

Avery's beautiful young wife came to the door of the kitchen and smiled at Clint.

"I saw him walking up the beach," she said. "I have already put on some extra huevos. Good morning, Clint."

"Morning, Lita," Clint said.

"Husband," she said, "take our guest out onto the porch. I will serve you there."

"Damn right you will, woman!" Avery said with a laugh. "You'll serve us both!"

"Go!" she shouted, shooing him away with her apron.

They went back out to the porch, where they sat down in heavy wooden chairs at a wooden table. The house, the chairs, and the table had all been built by Avery Castle. As expert as the construction was, Avery was not a carpenter by trade. He was a gunsmith, and an old friend of Clint's. When Clint had decided to come down to the Mexican coast, he figured to see Avery, but he didn't figure to find his old friend with a young wife. And a pregnant young wife, to boot.

Lita came out of the house, her swollen belly preceding her, carrying a tray with a coffeepot, two cups, and a basket of fresh-baked muffins.

She poured them coffee and kissed her husband's head while he caressed her belly. She was beautiful with her hair being blown by the wind off the ocean.

"I will be right back," she promised.

"How'd you get so lucky, Avery?" Clint asked.

"I don't know," the older man said. "I don't know what she sees in me."

"No, I mean this coffee," Clint said. "It's wonderful. How did you get so lucky to find a woman who could make great coffee?"

Avery laughed.

"Have you decided?" he asked.

"Decided what?"

"When you're leavin'?"

"Oh, that," Clint said. "No, I haven't. I'm not in a hurry to get back to the U.S. I like it down here."

"So do I," Avery said. "But be careful. "I came down here five years ago, and I never left. I built this house, and found that woman. And now we're having a child."

"Why did you come down here?" Clint asked. "You never told me."

"Oh," Avery said, looking out at the ocean, "I don't even think I remember. All I know is, this is my home. And you're welcome to stay as long as you like. Uh, I mean in town, not here at the house."

"Don't worry," Clint said, "I'm not about to invade your little love nest."

"Good," Avery said, "then I guess I won't have to shoot you."

"That's good, too."

Lita came out carrying trays of food. She set them on the table, where the steamy smell made their mouths water. She went back to the kitchen, returned with three plates, then sat down with them and said, "Breakfast is served."

They dug in . . .

Rydell and Chance drank their beers, ate their food, and ignored the other men in the cantina, who also ignored them. The same could not be said for the women, however.

The younger girl at the end of the bar kept throwing hot glances Hal Chance's way, and he was extremely happy about it.

Rydell preferred the older woman, who while serving them their food had bumped her hip against his shoulder several times—a very firm hip. She also smelled of something both sweet and sour at the same time. Oddly, it was the sour—which may have been her sweat—that he liked better.

During the course of their meal, the younger woman

made her way to their table, and before long, Chance was
eating with one hand while he had the other around her
waist. Her name was Belinda, and she had an arm around
Chance's shoulder and was whispering in his ear when four
Mexicans entered, talking loudly.

They were arguing in Spanish as they approached the
bar. The bartender suddenly looked nervous as the four men
ordered whiskey.

Finally, one man looked around and called out, "Where
is my Belinda?"

The young woman stiffened and immediately tried to
walk away, but Chance held her tight.

"Where you goin', sweet thing?" he asked. "Stay here
with me."

"Gringo, you do not understand," she said. "That is
Rodrigo."

"Am I supposed to know who that is?" Chance asked.
"Rydell, do you know who that is?"

"Naw, never heard of him," Rydell said.

Rodrigo spotted Belinda standing with Chance's arm
around her waist.

"Chica," Rodrigo said, "come to your Rodrigo."

She tried again, but Chance held her fast. The bartender
looked worried again, and Belinda looked panic-stricken.

"You must let me go, gringo," she said, "or he will
kill you."

"Just relax, darlin'," Chance said. "He ain't gonna kill me."

"Then he will kill me," she hissed.

"He ain't gonna kill nobody," Chance told her. "Don't
worry about it. Whataya say, Cord?"

"I say we need more tacos."

THREE

Rodrigo huddled with his three compadres while the older girl, Raquel, came out with another platter of tacos for the two gringos.

"Who is this guy?" Rydell asked Raquel.

"He is a bad man, señor," she said. "And he considers Belinda to be his woman."

"Well, she don't exactly look like his woman right now," Rydell said. "What about you? You belong to anybody?"

"I belong to no man," she said.

"Good, then nobody is gonna come through the door and challenge me for you."

"No."

"Good."

"But they will kill you, señor," she said. "You and your amigo. You should leave."

"Don't worry," Rydell said. "Just get yourself to cover and wait for me."

"Sí, señor."

She hurried away from the table and into the kitchen.

"Get ready, partner," Rydell told Chance.

"I'm ready."

Eventually, the four Mexicans turned their backs to the

bar to face the two gringos. The bartender quickly vacated the area behind the bar. The other patrons in the place left their tables and sought cover. Two men actually flipped their table over and crouched behind it.

"Hey, gringo!" Rodrigo yelled.

The two Americans assumed he was speaking directly to Chance.

"You talkin' to me?" Chance asked.

"Sí, you," Rodrigo said. "You have your arm around my woman."

"Do I?" Chance looked around. "I don't see your woman here." He squeezed her. "Only mine."

"You are very funny," Rodrigo said. "Do you know who I am?"

"No idea," Chance said.

"I am Rodrigo Saltillo Maria Castellanos."

"Still never heard of you."

"I am what you gringos would call a bad man," Rodrigo said proudly.

"Well," Chance said, "I can see that you're an ugly man. But you'll have to prove you're a bad man."

Rodrigo Castellanos was, indeed, an ugly man. The teeth he had that were not gold were black, and he had many facial scars. This indicated to Rydell and Chance that the man was probably a knife fighter. He wore two pistols, a bandelero, and several knives. The men with him, each uglier than the one before, were similarly armed.

"Ho, ho," Rodrigo said to his friends, "it sounds like the gringo thinks he is a bad man. But maybe not as bad as Rodrigo, eh?"

They all laughed.

"What do you say, gringo?" Rodrigo asked. "Are you as bad as Rodrigo?"

"Probably," Chance said. "What do you think, Cord?"

"Probably badder," Rydell said.

"Then we shall prove it," Rodrigo said. "We will fight for Belinda."

"Fight for a woman?" Chance asked. "There are lots of women, Rodrigo. Go and find another one."

"I am afraid, señor, that I want this one."

"Well, amigo, I've got this one," Chance said.

"So we will fight," Rodrigo said, "with knives. The best man gets the girl, eh?"

Chance looked at Rydell, who nodded.

"Okay," Chance said, "we'll fight for her." He finally released the girl, who ran for cover. Chance stood up from the table.

Rodrigo smiled and took two of his knives out of their sheaths.

"I think you should use knives," Chance said, "but I'll use my gun."

He drew his gun and shot Rodrigo Castellanos in the chest. Rodrigo's mouth opened, his eyes popped, and he fell over. The knives fell from his hands and clattered to the ground.

The motion froze the other three Mexicans, and by the time they started for their guns, Rydell was also standing, and he and Chance were both firing. The Mexicans went down in a hail of lead.

Chance walked over to Rodrigo's body, kicked it once to make sure he was dead, then looked around the room, spread his arms, and said, "I win."

At that moment another man entered the cantina, gun in hand. Chance turned and quickly fired. His bullet hit the man in the chest, knocking him over.

Rydell walked over to the new dead man and looked down at him.

"Whoops," he said, looking at his friend. "*El jefe.*"

"What?"

"You killed the local sheriff, partner," Rydell said. "Looks like we can forget about spending time with these señoritas."

FOUR

Clint and Avery finished eating, but were working on a second pot of coffee.

"What has you so pensive, my friend?" Avery asked.

Clint decided to tell Avery what had been on his mind so much of late. The older man listened intently, not interrupting.

"You're a strange man," he said when Clint was done.

"How so?"

"You don't mind when people try to kill you because of your reputation," Avery said, "but you're upset that they're tryin' to kill you because of something more personal."

"That does sound odd," Clint said, "but it's right."

"Do you have any idea who's behind it?"

"When Travis came after me, it was very personal," Clint said. "After that it was hired killers, and no, I don't know who it was."

"How will you find out?"

"The next set of killers he sends," Clint said, "I'll make sure to take one alive."

"In tryin' to take a killer alive," Avery said, "you could end up getting yourself killed."

"That's true," Clint said, "but it's the only way I'm going to find out."

"Well," Avery said, "I wish you luck."

"Thanks."

Avery looked down at the beach and said, "Soon there will be a child running around down there, playing." He looked at his friend. "Maybe more than one."

"You think Lita's carrying twins?" Clint asked.

"No, I mean we will have more," Avery said. "Many, many more. A passle of kids."

Clint didn't say anything.

"You think I'm too old to have a passle of kids?" the older man asked.

"To tell you the truth," Clint said "I thought you were too old to have one, but you proved me wrong. So I wouldn't bet against a passle."

Avery laughed.

"Five boys and five girls," he said.

"Who has five boys and five girls?" Lita asked, coming out of the house. "Who has ten kids?"

"We're gonna have ten kids," Avery said.

"Oh no," she said, "and are you going to help carry them?"

"Not me," he said, putting his arm around her and holding her close, "I'm an old man."

"Not so very old," she said, leaning over and rubbing her nose up against his.

"I think I should be going," Clint said, sliding his chair back.

"No, no," Lita said, "stay."

"No, I've got to get back," Clint said.

"I thought you were down here doin' nothin'," Avery said.

"Well, that's right," Clint said, standing up, "but I've got a lot of nothing to do."

"You should let me find you a girl while you are here," Lita said.

"That's okay, Lita," he said, "I found a girl in town."

"That is not a girl," she told him. "That is a puta."

"She can't be a whore," Clint said, "because I don't go to whores."

Lita looked embarrassed, disengaged herself from her husband, and went inside.

"Sorry about that," Avery said. "Lita doesn't like the woman you've chosen to spend time with."

"What does she have against Carmen?" Clint asked. "She's a waitress, not a whore."

"Who knows what these women think?" Avery asked.

Clint shook hands with Avery.

"Come by again," Avery said. "For supper next time."

"I'll be back," Clint said. "I promise."

He waved and went down the stairs to the beach.

FIVE

Rydell slapped Raquel's big ass, then flipped the woman over and pawed her equally fulsome breasts. He leaned down to bite her dark brown nipples while she wrapped her fingers in his hair.

"You are not worried about killing five men?" she asked. "Including the sheriff?"

"Well," he said with his face between her tits, "I did think we'd have to leave right away, but the sheriff's dead. Who do we have to worry about?"

He kissed her then, roughly, her lips already swollen from other brutal kisses. He was a brutal man, and she knew she would be bruised when he was finished, but she would also know for days to come that she had been taken by a man, and not one of Rodrigo's filthy bandidos.

Rydell roughly spread her meaty thighs, positioned his swollen cock at the moist lips of her pussy, and then drove himself into her, causing her to gasp.

She clutched him to her with her arms and legs as he proceeded to fuck her hard . . .

* * *

Down the hall, Chance was doing much the same to little
Belinda, who had been excited by all the shooting, especially
since it had been over her.

Chance carried her into the room, her arms and legs
wrapped around him, her breasts pressed to his chest, her
mouth nibbling his neck.

"You killed them," she said breathlessly, "for me."

"I killed them over you," he said, "but for me."

He dropped her on the bed and roughly stripped off her
clothes. Her darkness inflamed him—dark brown nipples,
dark skin, and dark, bushy hair between her legs. He pulled
off his boots, dropped his pants and drawers, and leaped onto
the bed with her. In moments he had driven his hard cock
into her and was taking her in hard thrusts. She pulled off
his shirt and then held on tight to him, her teeth sinking into
his shoulder.

Over her own cries, Belinda could hear Raquel crying out
from her room down the hall, and that excited her even more.
Her excitement soaked into the sheets beneath them . . .

Rydell and Chance had agreed they had nothing and no one
to fear, now that the sheriff was dead. They had asked the
bartender if there were any deputies and he had shaken his
head no.

"Well," Rydell said, "we ate, and we did some shootin'.
We might as well do what we came here to do."

They had each grabbed a woman by the arm and pulled
them into the back hall.

When they were done, they met each other at the bar and
had a beer. The cantina was empty, except for the bartender,
who still looked worried.

"You sure had that gal screamin' her head off, Cord,"
Chance said. "I could hardly hear mine at all."

"I could hear yours," Rydell said. "She had a big voice
for a little gal."

"And she was a wet one, lemme tell you," Chance said. He drank half his beer down and looked around. "Where is everybody?"

Rydell looked around, too, then turned to the nervous bartender.

"Que pasa?" he said. "What's goin' on?"

"Señor," the man said, "I am just a poor merchant."

Rydell put his beer down and grabbed the man by the front of his shirt.

"What's goin' on?" he demanded again.

"T-They are outside, waiting for you."

"I thought you said there was no deputies."

"They are not deputies, señor," the man said, "they are just . . . citizens."

"Gonna try to bushwack us on our way out, eh?" Chance asked.

"*Lo siento*," the man said. "I am sorry, señor, but . . ."

Rydell released the man and looked at Chance.

"Well, partner," he said, "you better make sure your gun is loaded."

"My gun is always loaded, Cord," Chance said, "you know that. How do you want to play this? Just walk on out?"

Rydell rubbed his jaw, looked at the bartender again.

"How many men out there?"

"Perhaps *seis*," he said.

"Six," Rydell said.

"They any good with guns?" Chance asked the bartender.

"As I said, señor," the man answered, "they are citizens, storekeepers." He shrugged. "They shoot like storekeepers."

Chance looked at Rydell and grinned.

"Whataya say, partner?" he asked. "Just walk on out there?"

"Why not?" Rydell replied. "We can use the practice."

The two gunmen stepped out of the cantina, their hands on their belts.

"Where are they?" Chance asked.

"Maybe they changed their minds," Rydell said.

"Cowards," Chance said. "First they want to bushwhack us, and then they changed their minds?"

"Well, remember what the bartender said," Rydell replied. "We're dealin' with storekeepers."

"They could be waitin' until we step into the street," Chance said.

"That's possible," Rydell said. "I'll watch the rooftops, you watch the doorways across the street."

"Okay."

Together they went to the edge of the boardwalk, then stepped down into the street, as if to mount up.

Rifle barrels appeared on the rooftops and from doorways and windows across the street.

"Got 'em?" Rydell asked.

"I got 'em."

"Let's do it."

Chance smiled. Both men drew their guns and started firing with deadly accuracy.

SIX

It didn't take long.

The storekeepers not only shot like storekeepers, they were inept. Several of them fell from the rooftops when they were hit, while others staggered out the doors, or fell through the windows.

The bartender was foolish enough to come running through the batwing doors carrying his rifle, so Chance turned and shot him as well.

Then it was quiet.

The two gringo gunmen ejected their spent shells, reloaded their guns, and holstered them.

They looked at their horses. The Mexicans were such bad shots even the horses had not been hit.

The two men mounted up and looked around. The two girls came to the batwing doors. They didn't seem to be upset by all the bodies, or even the body of the bartender lying right in front of the doors.

"*Vaya con Dios*," Raquel called out, and both of the women waved.

"What a town," Chance said.

Rydell agreed with a shake of his head.

"If all Mexicans shoot like this, we won't have any trouble takin' our man."

"When we find him," Rydell reminded his partner.

"I'm leavin' that part up to you, partner," Chance said. "I got confidence in you."

"Appreciate that, Chance."

Chance looked behind him as they rode out of town.

"If all the Mexican women are like those two . . ."

"I know what you mean," Rydell said with a smile.

Clint sat in a chair in front of his hotel and watched the people go by. It was the way he had spent most of his days since coming to town. That is, except for the time he spent on the beach, either walking or visiting his friend Avery.

He was glad to find his friend so happy, but wondered how much further Avery would be able to go after this first child was born. Avery had never seemed like the kind of man who wanted kids. Clint himself had never had the urge to father one child, let alone a brood. He hoped Avery wouldn't be too disappointed if there was just the one.

He had never regretted not having fathered any children. It was just not in the cards for the Gunsmith.

SEVEN

Clint was still sitting in front of the hotel when Sheriff Domingo Vazquez came walking up to him.

"Señor Adams."

"Sheriff," Clint said. "Care to join me?"

"I do not mind," Vazquez said. He pulled another chair over and sat next to Clint. He took two cigars from his pocket and handed one to Clint, then held a match for him before lighting his own. Clint did not smoke much, but rarely turned down a free cigar.

"Gracias, amigo," he said.

"*Por nada*," Vazquez said.

When Clint first came to town, Vazquez had braced him, advising him that he would not stand for trouble in his town, not even from the American legend called the Gunsmith. Clint had promised the man he had no intention of causing any trouble.

To the sheriff's surprise, Clint had kept his words, had avoided trouble at all costs. During the course of his stay, the two had formed a tentative friendship, occasionally sharing a cigar or a drink.

"It has been very quiet of late," Vazquez said.

"Don't you like it when it's quiet?"

"Not at all."

"Why not?"

"It usually means something bad is going to happen," Vazquez said. "I prefer to have a little trouble each day. I can handle that."

"You seem to me the kind of man who can handle any kind of trouble."

Vazquez was a handsome man in his late thirties, with a small, well-cared-for mustache and—when he wasn't wearing his sombrero—slicked-back black hair. He carried himself with the air of a confident man—never more so than when he had braced Clint the first time. Clint had sensed that while the man was careful, he was not afraid.

"Ah," Vazquez said, you flatter me, señor. I do my job, to be sure."

"Perhaps that is why it's so quiet," Clint suggested.

"Sí, perhaps," Vazquez said. "It may also be because you are here."

"Me?"

The lawman nodded.

"Sí," he said, "many of the townspeople are afraid of you. They are afraid if they cause trouble, you will step in."

"I've never given any of them reason to fear me," he said, "and stepping in when there's trouble is your job, Sheriff, not mine."

"Indeed it is, señor," Vazquez said. "I am simply telling you what I hear."

"Well, I'm sorry to hear that," Clint said. "Maybe I should be on my way and allow you to have your days of little trouble."

"It is too late for that, señor."

"How do you figure?"

"There have already been many quiet days," Vazquez said. "Certainly there is big trouble coming. I do not know when, but it is surely coming. That is my experience. So you see, should you decide to leave, it would not solve the problem."

"Why are you telling me all this?" Clint asked.

"I was just looking to pass the time with some conversation, señor," Vazquez said. "And perhaps invite you to dine with me this evening."

"I appreciate the offer, *Jefe*," Clint said, "but I already have an invitation to dine."

"Ah, the lovely Miss Garcia?"

"Actually no . . ."

"Then your good friend who lives on the beach?"

"Yes." Avery had told him to come back "next time" for supper. He was simply stretching the point.

"Then I will not try to tempt you away," Vazquez said, rising. "Perhaps another evening?"

"Perhaps," Clint agreed.

"Very well," Vazquez said, "then I wish you a good rest of the day."

"Thank you for the cigar."

"*Por nada*, señor," Vazquez said.

The sheriff walked away and Clint wondered if there had been something else in that conversation besides the obvious.

After Vazquez left Clint, he walked to the Cantina Carmelita and entered. He went to the bar and ordered a beer. Before long, the owner of the drinking and gambling establishment came over and joined him.

"And so?" Ernesto Paz asked.

"He will not be leaving anytime soon."

"That is good, isn't it?"

"It can be, I suppose."

"Why would he leave?" Paz asked. "No one bothers him, he has a woman, and a friend . . . perhaps two friends?"

"You flatter me, Ernesto," Vazquez said. "Clint Adams

is much too careful to make friends so quickly. I would say we have a careful, cordial relationship."

"Well, whatever it is, you'll have to take advantage of it when the time comes."

Paz turned and walked away. Vazquez watched until the man entered his office, then turned and left without finishing his beer.

EIGHT

For his supper, Clint went to the small Rosa's Cantina—
which served only food, not liquor or gambling—where
Carmen was a waitress.

"I wondered if you were coming tonight," Carmen said
with a smile.

"Any tables available?" he asked.

They looked around. In point of fact, there were only two
tables that were taken.

"I think we can seat you, sir," she said, playing along.
"Would you like your regular table?"

"That would be fine."

Smiling, she led him to a small table against the back wall.

"Coffee?" she asked.

"Sí."

"I will be right back."

She went to the kitchen and returned momentarily with
a pot of coffee and a white mug. She poured steaming black
coffee into the mug for him and then asked, "What would
you like for your supper?"

"What is Rosa preparing tonight?" he asked.

"Whatever you want, señor," she said. "You are a special
customer."

"Steak?" he asked.

"Ah, with Mexican spices," she said. "I will tell her."

She returned a short time later with a perfectly prepared steak, redolent with Mexican spices, along with sweet onions, rice, and refried beans.

"Thank you, Carmen," he said.

"Do not thank me," she said. "Thank Rosa." She leaned in close and added, "You can thank me later."

She smiled again and left him to his meal.

While he was eating, a man entered, looked around, saw him, and walked over to him.

"Padre," Clint said.

"May I sit?" the man asked.

The tall, slender man dressed in black sat down across from Clint. He had a long face made longer by age and the fact that he once weighed many more pounds. Despite the weight loss, though, Clint had recognized him on the street one day. And the man knew it. That was almost a week ago, and this was the first time the man had approached him since.

"What name are you going by?" Clint asked.

"Father Flynn."

Clint smiled.

"What's funny?"

"An Irish priest in a Mexican town."

"This was as far away as I thought I could get."

"From what?"

"My old life."

"I see. Would you like some coffee?"

"Yes, I would."

Clint waved to Carmen. She brought another cup and poured it full.

"Anything else, Padre?" she asked.

"No, thank you."

He did not speak again until she walked away.

"Is that what you're doing?" Father Flynn asked.

"Is that what I'm doing?"

"Hiding from your old life."

"I have only one life . . . Father."

"So then you're hiding from that one."

Clint chewed his steak and said, "Not hiding, actually. Just . . . taking a break."

"Well, I am hiding," Father Flynn said, "from a life I've left far behind me. When I saw you on the street last week, I knew you recognized me. My first instinct was to flee."

"Run away again? To where this time?"

"That was the question," Father Flynn said, sipping his coffee. "I couldn't think of anywhere to go, so I thought I would just talk with you."

"About what?"

"About what you would say about me when you return to the U.S.?"

"Why should I say anything?"

"Do people still wonder about me?"

"I'm sure they do."

"And you don't have any desire to tell anyone you found me?" Father Flynn asked. "To a friend maybe?"

"No," Clint said.

"Can I believe that?"

"We were never friends, Father," Clint said, "but I think you know that I keep my word."

The priest put his coffee cup down and stared across the table at Clint.

"Yes, I do know that," he said. "I'm sorry."

"No apology necessary."

Father Flynn pushed his chair back and stood up.

"Will you come to my church?" he asked.

Clint swallowed the piece of steak he'd been chewing and said, "Let's not push it, Father Flynn."

NINE

Clint finished his meal, promised to return when Carmen was ready to go home. They would either go to the small house she had at the north end of town, or to his hotel room.

After leaving Rosa's, he went to Cantina Carmelita. It was the biggest place in town to drink, and it offered various forms of gambling. Clint, in an attempt to distance himself from his life for a while, had stayed away from the poker tables. All he did when he was there was nurse a beer or two, and relax.

"*Cerveza*," he said to the bartender.

"Sí, señor."

Clint had come a long way from home to find some peace, and so far, even though the people in town knew who he was, no one had tried him. Aside from a word or two with bartenders or waiters, he did most of his talking with Avery, Carmen, and Sheriff Vazquez.

Also Ernesto Paz, who owned the Carmelita.

While he was nursing his first beer, the well-dressed cantina owner came up to him and smiled broadly.

"Welcome, Señor Adams," he said. "Welcome back to my humble establishment."

In most U.S. towns, the Carmelita would have been considered humble, but not here in Laguna Niguel.

"You are very modest, Señor Paz," Clint said. "You have a fine place here."

"Gracias," Paz said. He was not tall, probably about five-nine, around forty years old, and always impeccably dressed. "Would you consider playing some poker tonight? I can promise you some good competition."

"No, thank you," Clint said. "I'm not playing much these days."

"Understood," Paz said, putting his hands up, palms out, "I will not try to pressure you."

"Thank you."

"But if you should change your mind," Paz added, "I would be happy to arrange a private game."

"I'll let you know, Señor Paz."

"Excellent," Paz said. "I will let you enjoy your beer in peace, then."

Paz pressed his hands together as if in prayer, and backed away.

Paz usually asked Clint once a day if he wanted to play poker. Clint had been refusing since he'd arrived there. You'd think the man would get the hint.

Clint was on his second beer when Sheriff Vazquez put in an appearance. He smiled and came across the room. The bartender had a beer on the bar by the time he got there.

"Gracias, Raul."

He took a big drink and smiled at Clint.

"Has Paz bothered you again about poker?"

"He asked."

"He is desperate to say the Gunsmith played poker in his establishment."

"Sorry I can't help him."

"I have told him that, but he does not listen to me."

"I was wondering something," Clint said. "I never asked you if you had deputies."

"*Por qué?*" Vazquez asked. "Do you want to be a deputy?"

"No, I was just wondering about this bit of trouble you're expecting."

"Well, I have two deputies," Vazquez said. "They are . . . how do you say . . . okay?"

"Yeah, okay," Clint said.

"But if, as you say, big trouble comes, I am not sure their guns will be very helpful."

"Uh-huh."

Clint was waiting for the lawman to ask him again about being a deputy, but the question didn't come. Instead, the sheriff eyed the crowded interior of the place while he finished his beer.

"Well," he said, setting down the empty mug, "things look quiet enough in here. I must get on with the rest of my rounds. Have a nice evening, señor."

"Thanks, Sheriff."

The lawman left and Clint turned his attention back to his second beer.

TEN

Clint was waiting out front when Carmen came out and locked the door of the cantina behind her.

"Where's Rosa?" he asked. "Why doesn't she lock up?"

"Rosa always leaves first."

"You know, I've never seen her."

"Oh, you don't want to," Carmen said. "She is very ugly."

"That's not nice."

"It is very true," she said. "She is a wonderful cook, but she looks so bad that she just stays hidden in the kitchen all day."

"That's a shame."

"She is very happy," Carmen said, linking her arm in his. "Where shall we go tonight?"

"My hotel," he said.

"Oh, good," she said. "I like your hotel room."

Actually, his hotel room was larger than her little house, but it was all she could afford on what she was paid at the cantina. Carmen was beautiful, but she wouldn't use her beauty to make money, not serving drinks or working in a cathouse.

They walked to the Hotel Especiale, which was the larger of the two hotels in town. Clint's room was on the top floor.

They walked through the large, well-furnished lobby to the stairs, and the clerk nodded knowingly at Clint.

"I love walking through this lobby," she said. "I just wish I was dressed nicer."

"You look beautiful."

They went up the stairs to his room. He unlocked the door and let her go in first. It was a two-room suite, the best the hotel had to offer, and the cost was a fraction of what it would have been in the States.

She turned around to face him and said, "I should take a bath."

"You can do that tomorrow," he said. "In the morning."

"But I smell like, well, food."

He walked to her, put his arms around her, and pulled her close. He could feel her warmth through her dress.

"I like the way you smell after work," he said, putting his nose in her hair.

"You just like me because I smell like steak," she said, snuggling up against him.

"You smell like Carmen," he said, "always."

She lifted her face to him and he kissed her, gently at first, and then more ardently. While he was kissing her, he worked her dress off her shoulders and down around her waist. Her full, bare breasts were hot and smooth. He kissed her neck, and her shoulders, worked his way down to her breasts, nibbled on her nipples. She sighed, held his head there. Her brown nipples swelled in his mouth.

He walked her to the other room, to the bed, where he sat her down and worked her dress off completely. She had a lovely, streamlined body, with small, rounded breasts and slim hips. She was an elegant girl who really didn't know it.

He kissed her, then stood up, removed his gun, and hung it on the bedpost. Carmen went to work on his trousers and before long had them down around his ankles. She took his cock in her hands, stroked it, leaned forward, and kissed it.

She moaned, licked him, and then took him into her mouth. She sucked him, rubbing her hands up and down his legs, taking his bare ass in her hands and pulling him to her so hard he staggered because his pants were around his ankles.

So she sat him down on the bed, removed his boots and trousers, then laid him on his back and straddled him. Dangling her pert breasts in his face, she took him inside her steaming depths and began to ride him. He moved his hips with hers, kept his hands all over her, and they moved faster and faster until he bucked her off, slipped her over, spread her legs, and drove himself into her. He grabbed her ankles, spread her even more, and fucked her while she spoke Spanish to him, inflaming him . . .

Later they lay together on the bed and she asked, "Did you see your friend down by the beach?"

"I did. I had a late breakfast with Avery and his wife. She's pregnant."

"She does not like me."

"Why do you say that?"

"Because she calls me a whore."

"No—"

"Oh, yes," she said. "I have heard her, my friends have heard her."

"Well . . . why?"

"I do not know," she said. "So please. Do not ever invite me to go there with you."

"Okay, I won't."

"But you must continue to see your friend."

"I will."

"He must be very happy about the baby."

"He is," Clint said. "I'm surprised he was able to do that, though. At his age. I think even he's surprised."

"We are not surprised about that in Mexico," she said. "Our men become even more potent with age."

"That's good," Clint said. "Maybe he caught some of that."

She slid her hand down between his legs and took hold of him.

"Hmm," she said, "I think perhaps you have caught it as well."

"Then let's test it out, why don't we?"

ELEVEN

Cord Rydell and Hal Chance rode through several more towns after their experience in El Diablo. They heard no news about the shootings there.

"Maybe news don't travel fast," Chance said.

"Suits me," Rydell said. "Whether we have to shoot it out again or not, suits me."

"These Mexicans sure can't shoot," Chance said. "Not the storekeepers or the bandidos."

"Well, so far we ain't met up with any Federales or lawmen," Rydell said.

"I don't think we'll have to worry much about them either."

"We'll see," Rydell said. "Don't kid yourself. I've run into some pretty good lawmen down here."

"Like who?"

"Never mind," Rydell said. "Just don't underestimate the law."

Chance laughed. "Like that lawman in El Diablo?"

"You never gave him a chance," Rydell said.

"Yeah, and that's the way I like to treat my lawmen. Make 'em dead."

"There's the cantina," Rydell said. "Let's see if we can get in and out without killin' anybody this time."

"Hey, I just need to find me a señorita—"

"No girls this time," Rydell said. "This is business."

"Ah, Cord—"

"You heard me."

"What if your man ain't there and we have to wait?" Chance asked.

"You can have food and drink," Rydell said, "no girls."

"Ahhh . . ."

They dismounted, tied their horses off, and went inside.

They stopped just inside the door and looked around. The place was almost empty, so it was easy to see that Rydell's man wasn't there.

"What if he don't come?" Chance asked.

"We'll wait," Rydell said. "He'll be here."

"How can you be so sure?"

"I am," Rydell said. "That's all you need to know. Come on."

Rydell led his partner to the bar and ordered them two beers.

With a mug in his hand, Chance turned and looked around the place. There were no girls on the floor. That suited Rydell, but not Chance.

"What kinda place has no girls?" he complained.

"Just relax," Rydell said. "I'm serious. We don't want no trouble this time."

"Hey," Chance said, "I ain't one who goes lookin' for trouble."

"No, I know that, Chance," Rydell said. "I know that."

They were working on their second beers when the batwing doors opened and a man stepped in. He looked around, spotted Rydell, and came walking over.

"Rydell," he said.

"Oates. Beer?"

"Oh, yeah. Who's this?"

"Lyle Oates, meet Hal Chance."

Oates and Chance nodded to each other, and Oates gratefully accepted a beer from the bartender. He immediately drank half of it down. He was in his thirties, with long, lank hair and sunken eyes.

"Ahhhh, that's good. Been ridin' for a while."

"You got somethin' for me, Oates?" Rydell asked.

"Yeah, I got somethin'," Oates said. "Your man's holed up in a beach town down south called Laguna Niguel."

"How far away?" Chance asked.

"Coupla days."

"But we're already near the water."

"It's still a coupla days away," Oates said. "The ocean's pretty big, pardner."

Chance looked at Rydell, who nodded.

"Pretty big," he agreed.

"Damn!" Chance said.

"You wanna ride with us?" Rydell asked Oates.

"What's in it for me?" Oates asked.

"Ride with us a while," Rydell suggested. "I think you'll like what you hear."

"And if I don't?"

"I'll pay you the same again, and you can be on your way," Rydell said. "But I think you'll want to come along."

Oates looked at Chance, and while he wasn't looking for any kind of affirmation, Chance nodded.

"Yeah, okay," Oates said, "but can we get somethin' to eat first?"

"Definitely," Rydell said, "but we'll be ridin' out as soon as we're done."

"No bed?" Oates asked.

"No girls?" Chance asked.

"Just food," Rydell said, "and then we'll be on our way."

They sat at a back table and had some burritos and beer.

"You see him?" Rydell asked.

"Huh?" Oates said with his mouth full.

"Did you see him in this town?"

"No, I didn't see him myself," Oates said. "Somebody else saw him."

"Who?"

"That don't matter," Oates said. "Just somebody I know."

"Can you trust him?"

"Huh?"

"Trust. Can you trust him?"

"Whataya talkin' about, trust? Men like us, trust don't ever come into what we do. Can you trust him?" he asked, pointing at Chance. "Can he trust you? Can I trust you?"

"Okay, okay," Rydell said. "Can you depend on his information?"

"Yeah, I can depend on his information."

"What about the local law?"

"He's no pushover, but his deputies are a waste."

"Okay," Rydell said, "okay, it sounds good."

"What about the guy?" Chance asked.

"What about him?"

"He got anybody around him?"

"Nobody we have to worry about," Oates said. "He's a sittin' duck."

Chance picked up his beer and said, "Here's to sittin' ducks."

TWELVE

Oates got up to leave the cantina first. He went to the batwings, looked outside, then turned and came back.

"I got bad news," he said.

"What?" Rydell asked.

"There are Mexican lawmen waitin' outside.

"How did that happen?" Rydell said. "How'd they know we were here?"

"They don't know you're here."

"Then what?" Chance asked.

"Well, they, uh, followed me here."

"They what?"

"Followed me."

"What for?"

"Well, I had some trouble on my way here."

"So you led them here?"

Oates shrugged and said, "I figured you'd help me out, you know? I mean, you want me to go with ya, right?"

"You're a sonofabitch, you know that, Oates?" Chance said.

"Yeah, I know that."

"All right," Rydell said, "so how many are out there?"

"Maybe half a dozen."

"We handled half a dozen in that little shit town," Chance reminded Rydell.

"Yeah, half a dozen storekeepers. This is different. These are—what kind of lawmen are they?" he asked Oates.

"Federales."

"Great," Rydell said. "Now we're gonna be on the hook for killin' a bunch of Federales."

"Look," Oates said, "we take care of these fellas, we go and get your guy, and then we hightail it back to the States. Easy as pie."

"Yeah, right," Rydell said. "Okay, look, Oates. You're gonna have to go out the front door."

"We're all goin' out the front, ain't we?"

"No, me and Chance are goin' out the back."

"And then what?"

"Chance and I will go around and come at them from both sides."

"What do I do?"

"Just go out the front and make like you're gonna surrender," Rydell said.

"Surrender?"

"Yeah, you know. Hands up? Then you draw your gun, and we'll be right there with ya."

Oates stared at Rydell.

"Cord . . . I can trust you on this, right?"

"Right," Rydell said. "We'll get this done and then you'll take us to—what's that town?"

"Laguna Niguel."

"Right, Laguna Niguel. Now go."

"Thanks, Cord."

Oates headed for the front door.

As the batwing doors opened, Capitan Huerta lifted his arm and told his men, "Get ready, hombres."

They raised their rifles.

The gringo came out the doors with his hands up.

"I'm surrenderin'!" he yelled. "See? My hands are up."

"Drop your weapon to the ground, gringo!" Huerta shouted.

"Yeah, okay," Oates said, and drew his gun.

Huerta dropped his arms and his men fired, riddling Oates with bullets. His bloody body fell to the boardwalk, blood soaking into the wood.

"What about our horses?" Chance asked Rydell.

They were behind the cantina, waiting for the shooting to be done.

"Don't worry," Rydell said, "we'll pick them up after they move the body."

"You sure that's all they'll do?" Chance asked. "They won't come lookin' for us?"

"They followed Oates here," Rydell said. "They ain't after us."

"I thought you here really gonna help him."

"Are you kiddin'?" Rydell said. "That idiot brought the Federales with him. We don't need that kind of trouble, Chance."

"Are you sure you know where Laguna Niguel is?" Chance asked.

"Don't worry. We didn't need Oates for anythin' else."

"I guess he was right."

"About what?"

"Not bein' able to trust each other."

"As long as you do what you're supposed to do," Rydell said, "don't worry about trust, Chance."

"I know," Chance said, "that ain't for guys like us."

THIRTEEN

When Clint came out of his hotel the next morning, he found Sheriff Vazquez waiting for him.

"Amigo," Vazquez asked, "have you had breakfast?"

"Not yet."

"Excellent," the lawman said, "we will have it together."

"Why?"

Vazquez smiled broadly, spread his arms, and asked, "Why not? I am inviting you to eat with me." He pointed to his chest. "My treat."

"Well, if that's the case," Clint said, "lead the way."

"Come, amigo, I will take you to a special place."

Clint stepped down from the boardwalk and followed the sheriff, who chattered amiably the entire way. Finally, they reached a small restaurant Clint had not yet been to, and didn't even know existed. It was on a small side street. As they entered, he saw that there were only five tables in the place.

"*Jefe*," a small, older waiter exclaimed. He embraced Vazquez warmly.

"Alberto," Vazquez said, "I have brought a friend to sample your food."

"Wonderful! Any friend of yours is welcome."

"Clint, this Alberto Del Rio, my friend," Vazquez said. "Alberto, this is Clint Adams."

"A pleasure to meet you, señor. Please, both of you, have a seat. I will bring coffee, no?"

"I say coffee, yes," Clint said. "And strong."

Alberto smiled and said, "The stronger the better, *es verdad?*"

"That's very true," Clint said. "Gracias."

The two men sat while Alberto rushed to his kitchen.

"Alberto prepares the best breakfast in town," Vazquez said, "Mexican or American."

"That's good to know," Clint said. "I've been eating as Rosa's."

"Ah, Rosa's is very good as well," Vazquez said, "but, Dios, that woman in ugly."

"That's what I've heard."

Albert returned with a coffeepot and two cups, then said, "What will you have, my friend?"

"I will have my usual," Vazquez said.

"A full Mexican breakfast," Alberto said happily. "And you, señor?"

"Well, I usually prefer steak and eggs, but since I'm a visitor here, I'll also have a full Mexican breakfast."

"Excellent! I will prepare it with great care."

Alberto went back to the kitchen.

"While he's preparing breakfast with great care," Clint said, "why don't you tell me what this breakfast invitation is all about."

"I thought perhaps it would help to solidify our friendship."

"Do we have a friendship?"

"Well, a budding friendship, then."

"So you want to be my friend."

"I would like to be your friend, yes," Vazquez said. "And would like you to be mine."

"And does this new friendship have anything to do with this big trouble you're expecting?"

"Perhaps," Vazquez said. "Or perhaps I am just a friendly person, eh? Ask Alberto."

"Ask me what?" Alberto asked. He appeared at the table carrying a basket of tortillas.

"Am I a friendly man, Alberto?"

"Oh, sí, *Jefe*, very friendly," the smaller man said. He returned to the kitchen. There were no other customers in the small café.

"Why," Clint asked, "do I get the feeling Alberto is afraid of you?"

"I prefer to think of it as respect," Vazquez said.

FOURTEEN

Alberto brought out platters of huevos rancheros, chorizos, burritos, enchiladas, jalapeño corn cakes, and more coffee.

Over breakfast, Clint said, "All right, tell me about this trouble that's coming."

"I do not know anything specific," Vazquez said. "It has been my experience that when it is too quiet, something is coming."

"That sounds more like a superstition than a feeling."

"Whatever you would like to call it, it is coming," Vazquez said.

"Are you getting your deputies ready?"

"I have talked to them, warned them to be ready."

"Are they practicing with their guns?"

"I hope so."

"You should be making sure they do, instead of spending time trying to recruit me."

"Perhaps you could help me with them."

Clint laughed, picked up a burrito.

"That would mean I let you recruit me."

Vazquez shrugged, picked up a corn cake, and popped it into his mouth.

"You cannot blame me for trying," he said. "I am only

trying to keep my town safe by using all the resources at my disposal."

"I'm not a resource, Sheriff," Clint said.

"So you have said," Vazquez said. "But I have the feeling if trouble starts, you will not stand by and watch."

"I could just leave town."

"You're not ready to leave."

Clint picked up a tortilla, filled it with eggs and meat, and rolled it.

"Not when the food's this good."

When the table was cleared and they were both stuffed, Alberto brought out some more coffee, and some tequila.

"Just to top it all off," he said. He poured the coffee into their cups, and a shot of tequila for each of them.

"Gracias, Alberto."

They both downed their tequila, then Clint sipped some coffee.

"Why do you go to see the gringo in the house on the beach?" Vazquez asked. "Señor Castle."

"He's an old friend of mine."

"So you came here to see him?"

"I came there to get away from the U.S. for a while," Clint said. "That he was here was a happy coincidence."

"And you were seen talking to the padre," Vazquez said.

"I might join his flock."

"You are a religious man?"

"Not so far in my life, but who knows?" Clint asked. "And I suppose you know about the waitress?"

"Ah, your friend, Carmen, from Rosa's," Vazquez said. "Yes, I know about her."

"So you know I have two friends and one acquaintance in town."

"I am just doing my job," Vazquez said.

"Well, I have to admit, you know more than I thought you did."

"I know that Señor Avery Castle is more than he seems," Vazquez said. "The fact that he is your friend supports that. I also know that Father Flynn is more than he appears to be."

"Really? What do you think he is?"

"I do not know," Vazquez said, "but I keep my eyes on him."

"You've got to have a lot of eyes if you're watching me, Avery, and Father Flynn. And the town."

"I do," Vazquez said, "I have many, many eyes at my disposal."

"Then why do you think you also need my help?" Clint asked him.

"Because, señor," Vazquez said, "I have many eyes, but no guns."

As they stood up to leave, Clint noticed that Vazquez did not pay for their food. When he started to put money down, Vazquez said, "Don't."

"Why not?"

"Alberto and I have an arrangement," he said. "To change it now would . . . confuse him."

Clint gave in, and they left.

Outside, Clint said, "Thank you for breakfast."

"We are better friends now, yes?" Vazquez asked.

"We're friendly," Clint said, "but we're not quite there yet."

Vazquez laughed.

"For now I will accept that, señor," Vazquez said. "I must go to work. What about you?"

"Me?" Clint said. "I think maybe I'll go to the beach."

FIFTEEN

As Clint walked up the beach to his friend's house, he saw Avery sitting on the deck with Lita. When they spotted him, they both waved.

As he mounted the stairs to the house, Avery laughed and said, "Back for more breakfast?"

"Oh, no," Clint said, "today I'm very full. A full Mexican breakfast, compliments of Sheriff Vazquez."

"The sheriff," Avery said. "What did he want?"

"He's trying to recruit me."

"For what?"

"To help him with some big trouble he's expecting."

"What kind of trouble?"

"That he doesn't know," Clint said. "He just says it's been too quiet for too long."

"Clint, will you have coffee?" Lita asked.

"I will always have coffee," Clint said to her, "especially yours."

She smiled and went into the house.

"Sit," Avery said, "tell me about your talk with the sheriff."

"He was trying to make friends," Clint said, taking a seat.

"To recruit you."

"And trying to impress me with his ability to do his job."

"How?"

"By telling me certain things about you, and Father Flynn," Clint said.

Avery sat up straight, was about to speak when Lita came out with the fresh coffee.

"Uh-oh," she said, "the men have stopped talking when the pregnant lady came out." She put the coffee down on the table. "I will leave you to talk about your secrets."

Avery waited until his wife was out of earshot.

"What did he have to say about me?" he asked.

"Just that you were more than what you seemed," Clint answered.

"That's all?"

"That's it."

"How would he know that?"

"He doesn't know anything," Clint said, pouring himself some coffee, and some for Avery. "He has a feeling, and he puts lots of stock into his feelings."

Avery relaxed visibly, picked up his coffee cup, and sat back.

"What else? What's this about Father Flynn?"

"He has the same feeling about him."

Avery frowned.

"Flynn came to town a couple of years ago," Avery said. "Several years after me."

"Anything funny about him?"

"No," Avery said. "He rode in wearing a collar, immediately took over the church, which had been abandoned up to that point."

"What kind of contact have you had with him?" Clint asked.

"Not much. I don't go to church. I've run into him a time or two at the mercantile when I'm picking up supplies, but that's it."

Clint sipped his coffee. He did not say a thing to Avery about "Father Flynn" and had not said anything to the priest about Avery.

"The sheriff hasn't said or done anything to spook you," Clint said.

"No," Avery said, "I have too much going here to get spooked. And I haven't done anything he can hurt me with. It's just that I've tried to keep a low profile. I don't know what he's basing his feeling on."

"Well, I could cultivate this newfound friendship and try to find out."

"Anything you learn would be appreciated, but don't put yourself out on my account."

"No problem," Clint said. "The sheriff is always anxious to talk with me."

"Tell me," Avery said, "if this big trouble he feels is coming does show up, what will you do?"

"I don't know," Clint said, standing up. "Like I told him, I might not even be here. Tell Lita thanks for the coffee."

"You'll come back some night for supper?" Avery asked.

"Definitely."

"Anytime. Don't wait for an invitation. Lita cooks lots of food."

"Okay," Clint said. "I'll be here."

Avery nodded and Clint went down the ladder, walked along the beach back to town.

The church was still in need of repair, even though Father Flynn had taken it over after it was abandoned, and had been working on it.

As Clint entered, he saw the gaunt priest up near the altar, using a rag to clean some candlesticks. The church had a high, arched ceiling, many stained glass windows, a chipped and damaged crucifix over the altar, as well as chipped icons around the sides. Even in a state of disrepair, it was a beautiful building.

He made his way down the center aisle.

SIXTEEN

"Welcome to the house of God," Father Flynn said.

"Still got those good ears, I see."

Father Flynn turned around to face Clint.

"Old habits die hard. What brings you to God?"

"Not so much God as you," Clint said. "Is there someplace we can talk?"

"The sacristy," the priest said. "Come with me."

Still carrying the cleaning cloth, Father Flynn led Clint away from the altar and into the small room behind it where he usually dressed for mass.

"A drink?" he asked, setting the cloth down.

"Sacramental wine?" Clint asked.

"Whiskey."

"I'll have one, thanks."

Father Flynn opened a cabinet, took out a bottle and two shot glasses. He filled the glasses, returned the bottle to the shelf, and closed the cabinet. He handed Clint a glass and stepped back.

"What's on your mind?"

"I had breakfast with the sheriff today."

"Vazquez," Father Flynn said, nodding.

"Have you had much contact with him?"

"No, for obvious reasons, I think."

"Well, he's expressed an interest in you."

"Has he? Me or Father Flynn?"

"Well, that part of the conversation was about Father Flynn," Clint admitted.

"What did he say?"

"That he thought you were more than you seemed to be."

"That's all?"

"That's it."

"What's he base that on?"

"A feeling."

"And what did you say?"

"That we were acquainted—he already knew we'd talked—but that I didn't know anything about you."

"Thanks for that." He drank his whiskey, put the glass down. Clint wondered if he'd go for the bottle again, but he didn't. He finished his own and also put the glass down.

"I just thought I'd come by and let you know."

"I appreciate the information," Father Flynn said. "It's not going to change my life any, but it's good to know."

"The sheriff wants to be my friend," Clint said, "so I may be able to hear something else."

"If you do, and you're willing to pass it on, I'll be grateful to hear it. Come, I'll walk you out."

Father Flynn walked Clint to the front door of the church, and outside.

"*Buenas noches, Padre*," a woman said as she entered the church.

"Many of the locals are helping me clean the church up," Father Flynn said.

Clint could see several men working on the grounds in front of the building, assumed there were more unseen on the sides and in the back.

"Looks like you've found a home here, Father."

"It's starting to feel that way."

"What about the Church?" Clint asked. "I mean, the officials, or whatever—"

"The diocese is aware that I'm here."

Clint stared at the man. He'd assumed the collar was a dodge, but if the Catholic Diocese was aware of it, then "Father Flynn" must have actually been ordained.

"I admire the change in lifestyle," Clint said.

"It was that or die," Father Flynn said. "And I don't mean by the gun. I just had an epiphany that if I didn't change my life, I'd die and go to hell."

Clint had never had any such epiphany, but he admired the man for acting on his.

"Again, if the sheriff lets anything else slip, I'll pass it on."

Father Flynn shook hands with Clint and said, "Much obliged."

Clint nodded and walked away from the church. When he turned to look, Father Flynn had gone back inside. He hoped that nothing would happen.

He walked back to town.

"Come," Ernesto Paz said as someone knocked on his office door.

It opened and Sheriff Vazquez entered.

"Ah, Sheriff," Paz said, "have a seat."

Vazquez removed his sombrero and sat across from Paz.

"*Que pasa, amigo?*" Paz asked.

"I had breakfast with our new friend, Clint Adams."

"What was that like?"

"Cordial."

"Still doesn't agree to help?"

"Now he says he may not even be here."

"Is he planning to leave town?"

"No, he just said by the time the trouble came, maybe he'd be gone."

"Maybe the trouble won't come."

"Oh, it's on its way," Vazquez said. "My feelings are very rarely wrong."

Paz had to admit to himself that, in the past, the lawman's feelings had proven to be correct.

"I suppose we will have to just wait and see."

"I mentioned his friend Avery."

"And?"

"He did not even blink."

"He has not lived as long as he has by blinking," Paz said.

"No. I also mentioned the priest."

"Why?"

"They were seen together, and I have a feeling about the padre."

"You are having too many feelings these days, amigo."

"I would not argue that point," Vazquez said. "I do not like these feelings, Ernesto."

Paz took a bottle of whiskey and two glasses from his desk and said, "That makes two of us."

SEVENTEEN

"What's wrong?" Hal Chance asked his partner, Cord Rydell, as Rydell reined in his horse.

"Laguna Niguel is up ahead."

"So? Ain't that where we're goin'?"

"It is. I'm just thinkin' of the best way to go about this," Rydell said.

"The guy ain't gonna recognize us, right? We ain't never seen him, and he ain't ever seen us, right?"

"Right, but if we ride in together, two strangers, we might attract attention."

"And one stranger riding in, and then another, won't attract attention?"

"Yeah, it will," Rydell said. "That's why we're gonna make camp out here."

"And then what?"

"In the morning you'll ride in, get a hotel room, and relax. Walk around town. Take a look at the cantinas. And size up the local law."

"Okay, what about you?"

"I'm gonna scout around from out here, take a look at the beach. I'll ride into town two days after you."

"Okay, two days sounds good."

"We have a description of our guy," Rydell said. "If you see him, just find out where he's stayin', maybe even see what his daily routine is. But this is important, Hal."

"What?"

"Don't brace him alone," Rydell said. "I don't care what kind of advantage you think you might have, don't try to take him alone. If you mess this up, it's just gonna be harder in the end."

"Yeah, I get it."

"The other thing is, don't let him see you. If you're spotted, this is gonna be harder. Got it?"

"I got it. Why don't I just ride in now?"

"No," Rydell said, "I want to think about things overnight. I might come up with a better plan."

Chance was obviously impatient, but he gave in.

"Yeah, okay. I get it."

"Good. Now let's find a good place to camp, where we won't be seen."

Clint walked back to his hotel. Avery Castle and "Father Flynn" were entitled to live their own lives as they saw fit. He hoped that Sheriff Vazquez had no intentions of trying to change that.

He was not surprised that Laguna Niguel had become a destination for Americans who were looking to change their lives. He himself had drifted there, although he had no intention of staying permanently.

Rather than going into his hotel, he once again pulled up a chair and sat down in front. He wondered if Sheriff Vazquez's "feeling" about trouble coming was any more than that. Did the sheriff have some solid information that he wasn't giving out?

Was there a gang of bandidos on their way to loot the town? It wasn't likely Vazquez would go with two inexperienced deputies if that was the case. And he would try to recruit more than just one man.

Clint had convinced himself that the trouble Vazquez was expecting was, indeed, just a feeling and not based on anything solid.

He sat back, relaxed, and decided to spend the rest of the day right where he was, until supper.

EIGHTEEN

After Clint left Avery Castle's beach house, Lita came out and sat with her husband.

"Did Clint say something that disturbed you, my husband?" she asked.

He reached out and placed his hand on hers.

"Nothing for you to be alarmed about."

"Please," she said, "do not treat me like a child. If something is wrong, if there is a burden you must bear, let me help you."

"Lita," he said, putting his hand on her belly this time, not her hand, "you know I have a past."

"Yes, a past you do not wish to talk about," she said, "and I respect that. But if Clint said something—"

"He only said," Avery said, cutting her off, "that the sheriff believes that I am more than I seem."

"What does he mean by that?"

"He probably thinks that I am down here hiding from something in my past."

"But—"

"Yes, but I might be. But even if I am, he does not know what it is," Avery said. "There is nothing to worry about."

"Are you sure, my husband?"

"I am positive," Avery said. "We are going to live here a long time, my love, and raise many children."

She placed her hand over his, which was still on her belly. Then he slid his hands from beneath hers and said, "Now, go back into the house, woman. You probably have a messy kitchen to clean."

"Yes, husband."

She stood up and slowly walked inside the house.

Avery stood up, walked to another section of the deck, and entered the house through a different door. He went into a room that was his. Lita never entered it, not even to clean.

He closed the door behind him, opened the shutters on one window just to let a little light in. A wooden chest sat in a corner. He went to it, unlocked it with a key from his pocket. Right on top was a rolled-up holster. He took it out, unrolled it, and removed the Colt. It felt like an old friend in his hands, even though he hadn't wielded it for over five years. He'd cleaned it occasionally, just in case, but he had not used it.

He checked to make sure it was fully loaded. Hopefully, it would be able to remain in the trunk for years to come.

There was a time, years ago, before the house was built, when he'd stood on the water's edge, prepared to throw the gun out into the sea. But in the end he couldn't do it. So it went into the trunk—as it did now. He put the gun back in the holster, rolled it up, returned it to the trunk, closed the lid, and locked it. Maybe he should throw the key into the ocean, but that would have been an empty gesture. So he put it in his pocket and went back outside to finish his coffee. Maybe add a little whiskey to sweeten it.

After Clint Adams left, Father Flynn entered his office and locked the door behind him. He sat at his desk and silently cursed, then asked for forgiveness.

He had felt safe here until he saw Clint Adams in the street. Now Adams was telling him the sheriff was suspicious of him. Well, he was going to have to stick it out. He wasn't leaving, not when he had done so much work to change himself, and so much work on the church. Both of them had needed a lot of work, and neither was done yet.

Whatever happened, it would happen here, in his church.

There was a knock on his door. He got up, walked to the door, and unlocked it.

"Padre," Quintero Herrera said, "we have some questions about the roof tiles."

Quintero was a carpenter, and had been for forty years. He and his sons were helping Father Flynn renovate the church, and part of that job was repairing the roof.

"All right, Quintero," Father Flynn said, "I'll be right out."

Quintero nodded and said, "Sí, Padre."

Father Flynn closed the door behind Quintero, took a moment to compose himself, then opened it and followed the old man outside.

Rydell and Chance made camp in a clearing surrounded by rocks and trees.

"We won't be spotted from here, even when we make a fire," Rydell said. "Why don't you go and find some wood?"

"Yeah, sure."

While Chance hunted up firewood, Rydell unsaddled the horses, rubbed them down, and gave them what little feed they had in their saddlebags. The ground around there didn't yield much in the way of grass. He picketed the horses so they wouldn't wander off, and went back to camp. By that time Chance had a fire going, and a pot of coffee on it.

"Let's just do beans," Rydell said.

"Suits me," Chance said. "I'll be in town eatin' tacos tomorrow anyway."

"Sure," Rydell said "and in three days the job will be done, and we'll have all the food and girls we want."

Chance grinned and said, "That suits me just fine."

NINETEEN

As dusk came, Clint decided not to go to Avery's for supper—
not on this night anyway. He also didn't feel like going to
Rosa's. Instead, he decided to go where Vazquez had taken
him, to Alberto's place.

On the way there he passed the livery he had entrusted
Eclipse to. He hadn't checked on the big Darley Arabian in
a while, so he stopped in.

"Ah, señor," the elderly hostler said, "you are here to see
your magnificent animal? To see if I have cared for him
properly."

"Just stopping in for a visit," Clint said. "I wouldn't want
the big fella to think I forgot about him."

"He is in his stall, eating," the man said. "He eats more
than any two horses."

"He does have a big appetite," Clint agreed. "I'll just take
a look, let him know I'm here, and be on my way."

"As you say, señor," the hostler said. "Stay as long as you
like."

Clint walked through the stable until he came to Eclipse's
big behind in a stall.

"Wow, I never noticed what a big ass you have, boy," he
said, entering the stall, running his hand over the animal's back.

Eclipse ignored him and kept feeding.

"Yeah, okay," Clint said, "I know you're busy, probably sore at me for ignoring you. Tell you what, we'll go for a ride tomorrow. How about along the beach? Yeah, you'll like that. I'll come by and get you early." He stroked the big gelding's neck, then turned and left the stall, and the stable.

He retraced his steps from the day before when Vazquez had led the way, and found the little café.

"Ah, my new amigo," Alberto said when he entered. "Welcome."

Again the place was empty. Nervously, Alberto looked past him.

"Where is *el jefe?*"

"I'm here alone today, Alberto," Clint said. "Is that okay?"

"Of course, señor," Alberto said. "Of course."

"And I'll pay for my meal this time."

"Amigo, that is not nec—"

"Don't worry, Alberto," Clint said, putting his hand on the man's shoulder, "it'll be all right. Can you make me a steak?"

"American, or Mexican?"

"Surprise me."

"Coffee, señor?"

"The stronger the better."

"Then take a table, señor."

Clint grabbed a table against the wall and thought that Alberto seemed a lot more relaxed without Vazquez there.

The Mexican brought him a pot of coffee and a heavy mug, poured it full for him.

"Do you do everything yourself here, Alberto?" Clint asked. "Cook, and serve?"

"Sí, señor."

"Don't you get busy sometimes?"

"Never, unfortunately," he said.

"Then how do you make a living?"

"I make a meager living, señor, and it is very difficult," Alberto said. "But this is what I love to do, so . . ." He shrugged.

"And what about this arrangement you have with the sheriff?"

Alberto's eyes widened and he said, "I must see to your meal, señor," and rushed back into the kitchen.

After about two-and-a-half mugs of coffee, Alberto reappeared with a tray filled with food. He set it all down on the table in front of Clint and said, "Enjoy, señor."

Clint pulled the plate with the steak over to him and cut into it. It was juicy and red inside. He popped it into his mouth and chewed with great pleasure. Other platters were filled with potatoes, refried beans, corn cakes, and tortillas.

"Is it all right, señor?" Alberto asked.

"It's great, Alberto, just great. But I want you to sit with me."

"But, señor, you are a customer—"

"Don't give me that," Clint said. "Come on, sit."

Alberto hesitated, but then he pulled out the other chair and sat down.

"What's this between you and Sheriff Vazquez?" Clint asked.

Alberto frowned.

"I do not understand, señor."

"Why does he eat for free here?"

"He is *el jefe*," Alberto said, looking puzzled. "He eats free all over town." His frown deepened. "Is that not the way of it?"

"No, that is not always the way of it, Alberto," Clint said. "I wore a badge for a while when I was younger, and I did not eat free all over town."

"But, señor, who am I to change the way things are done here? *El jefe* wants to eat, I feed him."

"And what do you get in return?"

"Señor?"

"There must be something you get for feeding him for free," Clint reasoned. "Does he protect you?"

"But . . . he protects everyone," Alberto said. "He is *el jefe*."

Clint didn't think he was going to get through to the rotund little man.

"Does he frighten you, Alberto?"

"Oh, sí, señor," Alberto said, "but you must understand, I am a very frightened man."

"Do I frighten you?"

Alberto hesitated, then said, "Sí, señor."

"Alberto," Clint said, "I am going to pour you a cup of coffee, and then you and I are gonna have a long talk."

Alberto didn't know what to say to that, so he simply nodded and said, "Sí, señor."

TWENTY

"Tell me about the sheriff," Clint said.

"What would you like to know, señor?"

"Everything," Clint said. "Everything that you know about him."

"I do not understand, señor. Are you and the sheriff not friends?"

"We are not friends. We only met recently. I need to learn if I can trust him or not."

Alberto studied Clint for a long moment, then asked, "This is not a test, señor?"

"Not a test, Alberto. I'm being truthful."

Alberto seemed to breathe a sigh of relief that Clint was not friends with Sheriff Vazquez.

"Señor," he said, "the sheriff, he is a bad man."

"But he's the law," Clint said.

"That may be," Alberto said, "but that does not mean he is a good man. I give him free food because I am afraid of him. And there are many people in town who are also afraid of him."

"But why? What's he done to them? Or to you?"

"He is a deadly man with a pistol, señor," Alberto said, "and with his fists. I myself have seen him beat a man half to death."

"For doing what?"

"For not showing him the proper respect."

"Was the man a prisoner?"

"No, señor, just a citizen of Laguna Niguel."

"Then why is he allowed to keep his badge?"

"Even the town fathers fear him," Alberto said. "No one will try to take his badge."

"But in spite of this, does he do his job?" Clint asked. "Do the citizens of Laguna Niguel feel that he can protect them?"

Alberto thought a moment, then said, "I have to admit the answer is yes."

"If push comes to shove, can I trust him to watch my back?" Clint asked.

"I'm sorry, what is push and shove?"

"I mean, if anything happens, if there's trouble, can I depend on him?"

Again, Alberto took a moment to think about the answer before giving it.

"I think, señor, the sheriff wants something from you," he said, "so I believe you can trust him—until he gets it."

"That's very honest, Alberto," Clint said. "I appreciate that."

"Señor, can I ask you something?"

"Sure, go ahead."

"You are the Gunsmith, no?"

"I am the Gunsmith, yes," Clint said.

"Perhaps, señor," Alberto said, "when you and the sheriff have gotten what you need from each other, before you leave Laguna Niguel, you will . . . kill him?"

"I don't know about that, Alberto," Clint said. "I think if the town is afraid of Vazquez, and you don't want him around, you're all going to have to get brave and get rid of him yourself."

"Sí, señor," Alberto said. "I understand. But the sheriff does have a powerful friend in town."

"Is that right?" Clint asked. "Who would that be."

"Do you know Ernesto Paz?"

"I've met him," Clint admitted.

"He and Vazquez are friends, and Señor Paz puts all his power behind the sheriff."

"And just how much power does Señor Paz have?" Clint asked.

"He is the most powerful man in town."

Clint found that statement very interesting.

Clint thanked Alberto for his food and his words, and promised that Sheriff Vazquez would never hear what they had talked about.

"Gracias, señor," Alberto said. "I only hope I was able to assist you in some way."

"You assisted me in every way, Alberto," Clint said. "Thank you."

TWENTY-ONE

In the morning Rydell and Chance awoke and had coffee together. Rydell had some beans, but Chance was waiting until he got to town to have a real Mexican breakfast.

"Now, you understand what I want you to do, right?" Rydell asked.

"Yeah, Cord, I got it," Chance said. "I ain't stupid, you know."

"No, you ain't stupid," Rydell said, "but sometimes you do stupid things, Hal. Don't be stupid this time, because stupid is dead in this case."

What're you sayin'?"

"I'm sayin' no matter what happens, when you find our guy, stay away from him. Don't try to take him yourself. Don't let him see you. Just spot him, and wait for me. Got it?"

"How many times I got to tell you, Cord?" Chance asked. "I got it."

"If I get to town and find you dead, I'm gonna curse you all the way to hell, Hal."

"Don't worry," Chance said. "I won't be dead."

"But if you mess this up," Rydell said, "I'll kill you myself."

* * *

Clint awoke alone. Carmen had spent the night with him, but she had awakened early and slipped out. She needed to get ready for her job at Rosa's.

But the night before, prior to going to bed, he told her he wanted to talk to her about something . . .

"What is it?"

"Sheriff Vazquez."

"Domingo?" she asked. "What about him?"

"His first name is Domingo?"

"Sí. What about him?"

"I want you to tell me about him."

"Tell you what about him?"

"Whatever you know," Clint said. "He's been asking me for help, and I want to know if he's worth helping. How well do you know him?"

"I know him . . . very well," she said.

"Does that mean that you were once . . . involved with him?" he asked.

"It means I am always involved with him," she said. "He is my brother."

That stunned Clint. If she was Vazquez's sister, she would have to be loyal to him, and Clint didn't want her going back to her brother and telling him that Clint was asking about him.

"What kind of help does he want?" she asked.

"He says he senses trouble coming, and only has two inexperienced deputies to back him."

"My brother needs very little in the way of help, Clint," she said. "He is the deadliest shot with a gun I have ever seen."

"That's not always enough, Carmen."

"What do you mean?"

"Everybody needs help sometime."

"If my brother needs help, he knows where to get it."

Clint wondered if she was talking about Ernesto Paz. But

he didn't go any further with the questions now that he knew she was related to the lawman.

They went to bed . . .

In the morning Clint dressed and thought about what he had learned the night before from both Alberto and Carmen. If Alberto was to be believed, Domingo Vazquez was a hard man, and not a good one. But he did his job. And both Alberto and Carmen talked about his prowess with a gun. What Clint liked about Sheriff Domingo Vazquez that he had never alluded to that talent at all. He was, apparently, not one to brag.

Clint went down to the lobby, decided to have his breakfast in the hotel dining room. Over his steak and eggs he wondered who else he could talk to about Vazquez so that it wouldn't get back to the man.

He thought he knew of somebody.

Hal Chance rode into Laguna Niguel slowly, his eyes taking in both sides of the street. None of the citizens seemed to be paying him any special attention. If this had been an American town, he'd be noticed right away. The Mexicans were so much more relaxed about who entered their towns.

He rode until he came to a livery stable. Not knowing if there was another in town, he simply dismounted and walked his horse in.

"Ah, señor, welcome to Laguna Niguel," the old hostler said.

"Yeah, thanks," Chance said. "Like to put my horse up for a few days."

"Sí, señor, with pleasure," the man said. "Does your fine animal have any special needs?"

Chance's horse was a worn-out pony he'd taken from an Indian he'd killed. He'd be replacing it soon—whenever he saw another one he wanted to steal—so he said, "No, nothing special. Just rub him down and feed 'im."

"Sí, señor," the man said, taking the reins. "A few days, you say?"

"Probably."

"Enjoy yourself in our town, señor."

"Is there a cathouse?"

"Señor?"

"Whorehouse," Chance said. "Whataya call 'em here?" He held his hands in front of his chest, as if he were cupping melons. "*Putas?*"

"Oh, sí, señor, a very fine house," the man said. "It is at the end of the street."

Chance figured he could get directions from the hotel clerk so he said, "Yeah, fine."

He took his rifle and saddlebags from his horse, turned, and walked out, almost brushing shoulders with a tall man coming in. He didn't give the man a second look . . .

TWENTY-TWO

The man with the saddlebags brushed past Clint without a look or a word, so Clint gave him only a cursory glance. The hostler was leading a worn-out-looking pony to the back of the livery when he spotted Clint.

"Ah, señor, another visit!" he exclaimed.

"Go ahead and take care of that man's pony," Clint said. "I'm going to saddle my horse and take him out for some exercise."

"As you wish, señor."

Clint backed Eclipse out of his stall and saddled the big Darley, speaking to him the whole time. By the time he was done, the hostler was back.

"A magnificent animal, señor," he said, his eyes shining. "Magnificent."

"Yeah, he is." He turned to face the man. "What is your name?"

"I am Pablo, señor."

"Pablo, you wouldn't by any chance be related to Sheriff Vazquez, would you?"

"Related?" Pablo laughed and shook his head. "No, señor, thankfully not."

"Thankfully?"

The older man looked stunned that he had said that word out loud.

"Señor, I am sorry if the sheriff is a friend of yours—"

"He's not, I assure you," Clint said. "I barely know him."

Pablo looked relieved.

"Pablo, have you lived here all your life?"

"Oh, sí, señor," he said. "I was here when the town was just one adobe hut."

"What can you tell me about Sheriff Vazquez?"

Pablo frowned.

"How do you mean, señor?"

"I mean, what kind of man is he?" Clint asked. "What kind of lawman?"

"He is not a good man, señor," Pablo said. "I would be very careful if I was to consider taking him as a friend."

"And as a lawman?"

"He frightens people," Pablo said. "Perhaps this is a good thing for a lawman to do?"

"Perhaps," Clint said, "but not always."

"No, señor, not always."

"Thank you, Pablo," Clint said. "Thank you for talking with me."

"Sí, señor," Pablo said, "I hope I have been of some use to you."

Clint turned to leave, then turned back.

"Another couple of questions, Pablo."

"Señor?"

"Is the sheriff related to anyone else in town?"

"His sister, Carmen, works at Rosa's."

"What about Rosa?"

"Oh, no, señor," Pablo said, laughing. "She is much too ugly to be related to anyone."

"Anyone else?"

Pablo thought a moment, then said, "No, señor. Their parents died many years ago."

"What do you know about Ernesto Paz?"

A very serious look came over Pablo's face.

"Oh, señor, he is a very powerful man," the hostler said. "And very friendly with the sheriff. You must be very careful of him."

"And Paz?" Clint asked. "Is he close to anyone else?"

"No," Pablo said. "Oh, he has a woman in town, but she is just . . . his woman."

"And where would I find her—if I was looking?"

"She has a large house at the end of town, señor," Pablo said, "with many . . . girls in it. Do you understand?"

"I think I understand," Clint said. "Gracias, Pablo."

"*Por nada*, señor."

TWENTY-THREE

Clint decided to give Eclipse the treat he'd promised and took him for a ride on the beach. That meant he'd be riding him past Avery Castle's house.

He had not meant to be such a frequent visitor to his friend's house, but it really was a beautiful place to live, and Avery had such an air of happiness about him that he was a pleasure to be around, as was his wife, Lita.

This time, however, his intention was only to ride by, perhaps wave to Avery if he was out on his deck. However, after he turned Eclipse and rode back again, Avery was on the beach waiting for him.

"Come up for a drink," he said as Clint reined in. "That beautiful horse will be safe down here."

Clint nodded, dismounted, didn't bother to tie Eclipse off. The big gelding would not be going anywhere.

He followed Avery up to his deck, where his friend left him seated at the table, went into the house, came out with a bottle of whiskey and two glasses.

"I don't drink much anymore," Avery said, "but Lita allows me to have a glass with a guest."

"Ah, so this was a selfish invitation," Clint said, accepting a glass.

"Totally."

Avery sat down and sipped his whiskey.

"Well," Clint said, "maybe not totally."

"What's on your mind?"

"I've been checking into Sheriff Vazquez."

"And?"

"What I'm finding out isn't good," Clint said. "He seems to be a competent lawman, but not a good man in general."

"Who is?" Avery asked.

"You are."

Avery laughed. "You're forgetting about my past."

"No, I'm not," Clint said. "I'm just leaving it where it belongs, in the past."

"That's not always easy to do."

"Well, we're not discussing the past now," Clint said, "we're discussing the present. And from what I've heard, Vazquez has the town under his thumb. They fear him, and are so afraid they won't even try to fire him."

"Who have you been talking to?"

"Some locals," Clint said. "A man who owns a café, the hostler . . . Carmen, the waitress."

"Your waitress?"

Clint nodded, draining his glass. "Apparently, she is Vazquez's sister."

"You did not suspect this?" Avery asked.

"I never knew her last name."

"Ah." Avery poured more whiskey into Clint's glass, then refilled his own. "And why are you so interested in the sheriff?"

"Well, for one thing, he's interested in you," Clint said. "For another, he's been trying to recruit me for some 'trouble' that he feels is coming. He wants to be my friend."

"And he is not the kind of man you would take as a friend?" Avery asked.

"Well, I usually make up my own mind about that," Clint said. "Now, here I am talking to other people about him."

"Maybe you should go back to making up your own mind."

Clint finished his second glass of whiskey, waved off a third, and said, "Maybe you're right."

"What about the priest?"

"What about him?"

"The sheriff is interested in him, too, isn't he?" Avery asked.

"Another case of a man trying to leave his past behind," Clint said.

"But the sheriff is interested in him as well."

"And I warned him," Clint said. "You and I are friends, Avery. The priest, Father Flynn, he and I are two people who knew each other once. We were never friends."

"So if the sheriff decided to go after him, you wouldn't help?"

"I wouldn't help either one," Clint said. "I'd leave it to them."

"And if he comes after me?"

"I'll be here. Right by your side."

"I appreciate that," Avery said, "but I'm not so far gone, so old, that if one man comes after me, I can't face him, mano a mano."

"Sorry," Clint said, "not what I meant. Let me just say that I'd be here if you decided you needed me."

Avery nodded and said, "I appreciate that. I'll let you know."

Clint nodded and stood up.

"Thanks for the drinks," he said.

Avery stood up and walked Clint to the stairs, and down to the beach.

"Let me know what happens," Avery said as Clint mounted Eclipse again.

"I will," Clint said. "If something happens, you'll be the first to know."

TWENTY-FOUR

Chance stopped at a hotel and checked in, telling the clerk the same thing he'd told the hostler. That he'd be staying for several nights.

"Welcome, señor," the clerk said, handing him a key.

"Thanks." He took the key. "Can you tell me where I can get a good meal, a drink, and a woman?"

"All in one pace, señor?" the clerk asked, smiling in a knowing way.

"I don't care how many places I've got to go."

"I can direct you, señor . . ."

He went to his room, tossed his saddlebags in a corner, where he leaned his rifle against the wall, then sat on the bed and bounced. Might be too soft for sleeping, he thought, but good for fucking. He hoped the beds at the cathouse were good.

But first he needed to fill his belly with some good food. The clerk had given him several choices for good food. He was going to go to the closest one.

He left the room, visions of meaty tacos and burritos in his head.

                              *   *   *

Clint took Eclipse for another run on the beach, this time
in the other direction so that he did not pass by Avery's
beach house again.

When he brought Eclipse back to the livery, Pablo was
not around, so he unsaddled the horse and put him in a stall
himself. The horse immediately stuck his nose in his
feed box.

"See you later, big guy," Clint said, giving his rump an
affectionate slap.

He left the livery, walked from there to the sheriff's
office. Avery's advice was good, and it was something Clint
had been thinking about anyway. He should be making his
own mind up about Sheriff Vazquez, and not making any
decisions based on what others had to say.

He entered the office, hoping to find the sheriff sitting
behind his desk. Instead, he found a deputy there, cleaning
a rifle. The young man looked up as Clint entered.

"Hello," he said. "May I help you, señor?"

"I'm looking for the sheriff."

"As you can see, he is not here."

"Yes, I do see that," Clint said. "Do you know where he is?"

"No, señor," the deputy said.

"Then I guess I'll just keep looking."

As he turned to leave, the deputy asked, "Can I tell him
you were looking for him, Señor . . ."

"Adams, Clint Adams."

"Oh," the deputy said. He put the rifle down and said,
"Oh!" again, and stood up. "It is a pleasure to meet you,
Señor Adams. The sheriff told us that you were in Laguna
Niguel."

"Told you both?"

"Yes," the young man said. "I am Deputy Manuel Soto.
He told me and Deputy Julio Benitez."

"And what did he tell you about me?"

"He said that we should not bother you."

"In what way?"

"Well, we were both excited that we might meet the famous Gunsmith from America," Soto said. "The sheriff said we should not accost you, or gush."

"I see. Well, now you've met me."

"Sir," Soto said, "Julio will be very jealous."

"I'm flattered, Deputy," Clint said. "Have a nice day."

"Sí, señor," Soto said. "*Y usted.*"

Clint nodded and left the office.

Clint found Sheriff Vazquez at Cantina Carmelita, slumped over the bar relaxing, drinking a beer. It was still early, so there was little activity in the place.

"Beer," Clint said to the bartender, coming up alongside Vazquez.

Startled, the lawman straightened and looked at Clint.

"You move as silently as an Indian, señor."

"I think you were just deep in thought there, Sheriff," Clint said. "What was on your mind?"

"Hmm? Oh, nothing special. I was just . . . thinking."

Clint accepted his beer from the bartender and sipped it. Two whiskeys with Avery and now a beer. He was going to have to eat again soon.

"I went looking for you at your office," Clint said.

"Ah, so this is not a fortuitous meeting," Vazquez said. "I hope my deputy treated you with respect."

"Soto," Clint said, "he did, yes. He also told me that you instructed him and the other deputy, Benitez, not to . . . what was his word? Oh yes, 'accost' me."

"I simply did not want them gushing over you," Vazquez said. "That would be . . . undignified for my deputies."

"Oh, I see."

Vazquez leaned on the bar again, and Clint followed his example. The bartender moved to the other end of the bar. He never asked Clint to pay for his drink.

"Why were you looking for me?" Vazquez said.

"I've been thinking about what you said to me."

Vazquez grinned.

"I'm afraid I talk quite a lot, Señor Adams," the lawman said. "Which words are you referring to?"

"Just what you said about us getting to know one another better."

"Ah," Vazquez said, "I think what I said was that we should be friends."

"Well, I'm going to be in Laguna Niguel a bit longer," Clint said. "Maybe we should examine that possibility a little closer."

"Supper tonight, then?"

"Sure, why not? Someplace other than Alberto's, though."

"I know another place, señor," Vazquez said. "You will like it."

Clint drank his beer down to the halfway point, set the mug down on the bar, and then pushed himself upright.

"I'll meet you at your office," he said.

"Your hotel would be better."

"Okay," Clint said, "my hotel. At seven?"

"Seven is good."

"See you then."

The two men nodded to each other, and Clint walked out.

After Clint left the cantina, Vazquez finished his beer, then walked to the back of the room. He knocked and entered Ernesto Paz's office.

"Domingo," Paz said, sitting back in his chair. "Come in. Sit."

"Clint Adams was just here," Vazquez said, sitting across from Paz.

"And?"

"He was looking for me," Vazquez said. "He says perhaps we should explore the possibility of being friends. We are having supper together tonight."

"What do you think is on his mind?" Paz asked.

"I don't know," Vazquez said. "Carmen did tell me he was asking her some questions about me."

"Perhaps he has decided to ask the questions directly," Paz said.

"Perhaps."

"How is your lovely sister, by the way?" Paz asked. "You know, I still have a place here for her."

Vazquez stood and walked out.

TWENTY-FIVE

Chance left the small café with a pleasantly full belly. It had been weeks since he felt this well fed. Now, even though it was still kind of early in the day, he needed a beer to wash his food down.

He looked at the faces of the men he passed on the street, just as he'd examined the faces of the other diners in the café. So far he had not seen what he was looking for.

He went into a place called Cantina Carmelita and walked up to the bar.

"Beer," he said.

"Sí, señor," the bartender said.

As the bartender set the beer down in front of him, Chance saw a door open in the back of the room and a man stepped out. As the man walked toward the bar, he saw the badge.

Ah, Jesus, he thought. Rydell had warned him to keep a low profile. He leaned on the bar and tried to shrink himself down, which was hard since he was six-two.

"*Cerveza*," the lawman said to the bartender.

"*Sí, Jefe.*"

Chance could feel the lawman looking at him, but figured it was just because he was a stranger.

"Señor?"

He looked at the sheriff, who was staring at him.

"Do I know you, señor?"

"I don't think so," Chance said, staring into his beer. Rydell always told him not to make eye contact with a lawman.

"Just ride into town?"

"That's right."

"Do you plan on staying long?"

"I don't think so," Chance said. "I'm just passin' through, wanted to give my horse some rest."

"Well, we have a nice quiet town, señor," the sheriff said. "We would like to keep it that way."

Rydell also told him that the time came when you did have to look the law in the eye—especially when you were going to lie.

"Well, Sheriff." Chance said, looking at him, "I sure don't intend to cause any trouble."

"That is very good to know, señor." The lawman drank down half his beer, set the mug down on the bar. "Enjoy your time here."

"I will, thanks," Chance said.

The sheriff nodded and walked out of the cantina. Chance waved to the bartender to refill his mug.

The bartender brought him a fresh beer and said, "*El jefe* is a bad man, señor."

"Is he?"

"Sí," the bartender said, "*muy malo,* señor. I would stay away from him, if I was you."

"Thanks for the warning."

"*Por nada.*"

Cord Rydell poured himself another cup of coffee, drank it while staring out into the distance. He hoped Hal Chance wasn't in Laguna Niguel doing something stupid. Hopefully, he had just found himself a whore and was fucking whatever brains he had out.

He finished his coffee, poured another cup, wished he had a bottle of whiskey. He had no way to pass the time until morning, when he would also ride into Laguna Niguel. He was regretting the decision to allow Chance to ride in first. The man usually got himself in trouble—over women mostly—when Rydell wasn't there to guide him.

If he did anything to ruin this deal, Rydell would kill him.

TWENTY-SIX

Clint didn't know if having supper with the sheriff was a good idea, but he'd find out soon enough. If the sheriff was the man he'd heard he was, he'd wonder why Clint was suddenly willing to discuss being friends. Maybe everything would come out in the open over a steak.

And maybe it was time for Clint Adams to leave Mexico and go back to the United States.

Sheriff Domingo Vazquez walked back to his office, found Deputy Soto cleaning a shotgun.

"We must have the cleanest guns in town," he commented.

"I want to make sure they work if we need them," Soto replied.

"Well, they are clean enough," Vazquez said. "Go out and make some rounds."

"Yes, sir."

Soto replaced the shotgun on the wall gun rack, put on his hat, and left the office. When the sheriff gave him an order, he obeyed it without question.

Vazquez sat down behind his desk, opened a drawer, and took out a bunch of wanted posters from both Mexico and the United States. He leafed through them, looking for the man he'd talked to in the cantina. It was not that he recognized him, only that he recognized the type. But the man's face was nowhere to be found on the posters. Vazquez replaced them in the desk drawer, decided to go out and see which of Laguna Niguel's two hotels the man had registered in.

He left the office, unconcerned about leaving it empty.

Chance decided he wasn't going to learn anything by staying in the cantina. And he didn't want Rydell to think that he only got things done when he was being watched.

The bartender's advice was good, and he intended to keep it. He'd stay away from the law, whether it was the sheriff or a deputy. But he wanted to take a look around town, see if he could spot their guy so that when Rydell rode in, Chance would already know where their target was.

He paid for his beer and left the cantina. He stopped just outside the batwing doors, looking both ways and across the street. He decided to turn right and just take a stroll around town.

And maybe he'd end up at the cathouse.

Ernesto Paz sat back in his chair, watched the glass of brandy on his desk but didn't touch it. He hoped Sheriff Vazquez was handling this Clint Adams thing correctly. The opportunity was too important to make a mess of. Vazquez was competent in many aspects of his job, which was the reason Paz had engineered his route to the sheriff's job.

He picked up the brandy and sipped it. Laguna Niguel was his pond, and he was the big fish in it, but he was looking to move on. If Vazquez did his job correctly, he'd take the man with him as his right hand. A lot was riding on the way he handled this situation.

He rose from behind his desk, walked to the door, and

opened it. The bartender—this one was named Molina—was trained to sense when the office door opened, and he looked over. Paz waved to him, and the bartender left the bar and hurried over.

"Señor?" he said.

"Have you seen Santana?"

"Not today, señor."

"Find him," Paz said. "I want to talk to him."

"Today, señor?"

"Yes, today," Paz said. "As soon as possible. Now go!"

"Sí, señor."

Paz slammed the door. He didn't like any of his bartenders, but how much brains did it take to pour drinks? You took what you could get.

He went back and sat behind his desk.

TWENTY-SEVEN

Clint was sitting in front of his hotel when three men stopped in front of him.

"Señor," one of them said, "you are in my chair."

Clint eyed the three men. They were hard, looked like bandidos, wore guns as if they knew how to use them. Here it comes, he thought. Word had finally gotten around that the Gunsmith was in town. These three wanted to try him. Or had they been sent? Had they caught up to him all the way down here? The killers for hire?

No. He was far from home, and no one knew he was here, not even his friends Rick Hartman and Talbot Roper.

"Go away," he said to them.

"But," the middle one said, "I want to sit. I am tired."

The man smiled. He had several gold teeth in front, on top. Like the other men, he looked to be in his thirties. They were sweaty, dirty, weeks or months removed from their last contact with water and soap.

"Sit somewhere else," Clint said.

The man laughed, looked at his friends. They laughed, too.

"You must move, señor."

Clint wondered if they were willing to die over a chair. Or was he willing to kill them over a chair?

He was not.

"All right," he said, standing up. "You can have it."

The three men exchanged a disappointed glance. After a moment, they looked at him again.

"Never mind!" the middle man snapped. "I have changed my mind."

He turned and marched away, and the other two followed him.

Clint sat back down, puzzled.

Clint was still sitting out in front of his hotel when Sheriff Vazquez came walking up.

"*Buenas noches*," he said.

"Good evening."

"I hope you are hungry."

Clint stood up.

"I could eat."

"Come with me, then," Vazquez said. "We will go to my sister's restaurant."

"Your sister?"

"She does not own it," Vazquez said, "but she is a waitress there."

Could it be that Vazquez didn't know that Clint had a relationship with Carmen?

"Lead the way, then."

"*Bueno*."

Clint followed the sheriff to Rosa's. When they entered, Carmen turned, saw them come in, and smiled.

"*Hermano*," she said, rushing to her brother. "It has been a while since you came to eat here."

"I brought a friend," Vazquez said. "Or perhaps you already know him? Clint Adams."

"*Sí*," Carmen said, looking at Clint, "Señor Adams has eaten here several times. Nice to see you again, señor."

"And you, señorita."

The small cantina was doing a good business this evening, but there was an empty table in the back that she led them to.

"What will you both have?" she asked.

"Steaks," Vazquez said, "thick and . . . rare?" He looked at Clint.

"That's fine."

"And *cerveza*."

"Right away, Domingo."

"How is Rosa this evening?" he asked.

"She is fine."

"In good spirits?"

Carmen laughed.

"When is Rosa ever in good spirits?" She turned and went to the kitchen.

"Rosa is the cook and the owner," Vazquez said to Clint. "She is as ugly as sin. But you probably know that."

"I've heard," Clint said, "but I've never seen her."

"Believe me," Vazquez said, "you do not want to."

"I am kind of curious, though," Clint admitted.

"Well, then," Vazquez suggested, "walk into the kitchen and have a look."

Clint thought about it, and said, "Maybe not before my steak."

Vazquez laughed and said, "A wise choice."

During supper, Clint told Vazquez about the three men who had accosted him over a chair.

"I do not think they were interested in a chair, señor," Vazquez said.

"Do they sound familiar?" Clint asked.

"Sí," Vazquez said, "they sound like every bandido in the hills."

"Yes," Clint said, "they do, don't they."

"They had probably heard that the famous Gunsmith was

in town," Vazquez said. "Perhaps they were curious about you. You undoubtedly disappointed them."

"It was only a chair," Clint said.

"Sí," Vazquez said, "only a chair."

TWENTY-EIGHT

Vazquez managed to talk all through supper without really revealing anything about his character, or his life. Although he did talk about his sister, who he obviously loved very much. Clint felt there were veiled threats all through the conversation, should he hurt Vazquez's sister in any way.

Over coffee and sopapilla—a deep-fried pastry—Clint brought up the subject that was still on his mind.

"Are you ready to tell me what this big trouble is that you're expecting?" Clint asked.

Vazquez chewed on his pastry, seemed to be considering the question, then drank some coffee before answering.

"Some years ago I made an arrest, put some bad men away," he said.

"How many?"

"Three."

"On what charge?"

"Bank robbery, and murder."

"So they were put away for life?"

"They were sentenced to life in San Pedro Cholula City Prison," Vazquez said.

"So what's the problem?"

"They have escaped."

"All three of them?"

"The three of them, and several other men," Vazquez said. "They all escaped together."

"And you expect them to come here for you?"

"Wouldn't you?" Vazquez asked.

"I think so, yes."

"So you see," Vazquez said, "when they arrive, I have only my two deputies to support me."

"What about others from town?"

"Storekeepers," Vazquez said. "I can expect no help from them."

"What about Señor Paz?" Clint asked. "I'm told he's a very powerful man in Laguna Niguel. Can't he help?"

"Not personally," Vazquez said. "He is a businessman, of no use in the street."

"What about his money?" Clint asked. "Can't he hire some men to help you?"

"I am afraid Señor Paz has the same opinion that the other businessmen in town have," Vazquez said.

"That it's your job," Clint said.

"Sí."

Clint shook his head.

"Time and a different country, and nothing's changed since the last time I wore a badge," he said.

"I am afraid not," Vazquez said. "So you can see why I might try to take advantage of the fact that you are present in my town at this time."

"Do you have any word on whether or not the men have been spotted in the area?"

"No word at all."

"Isn't it possible they won't come?"

Vazquez gave Clint a look and said, "I suppose it is possible."

"Yeah, all right," Clint said. "Okay, what if they don't come until after I leave?"

"Then I will simply have to do the best I can," Vazquez said.

"What about you leaving town?"

Vazquez shook his head.

"That is not an option," the lawman said. "I am afraid I am cursed with a good portion of Mexican machismo."

"I understand," Clint said. "Many American lawmen have had the same affliction. Unfortunately, most of them are dead. Sometimes it's smarter to run."

"Would you run, amigo?"

Clint replied without hesitation.

"No, I wouldn't, but that's me," Clint said. "Running from a fight would only make me a larger target."

"Sí, that I understand."

They finished their desserts. Carmen cleaned the table, and poured them each some more coffee.

"Was the meal satisfactory, señors?" she asked playfully, as if they were strangers.

"Very much so," Clint said.

Vazquez took out two cigars and handed Clint one.

"Aye, Domingo," she said hastily, "do not light those up around me." She fanned the air and rushed away.

"She does not like cigar smoke," Vazquez said, striking a match and holding it out for Clint to light his cigar. He then used the same match to light his own.

"I got that," Clint said.

Vazquez puffed on his cigar until the tip glowed bright, then held it out and looked at it while smoke dribbled from between his lips.

"So, señor, now you know," he said. "What have you decided?"

"Sheriff—"

"Call me Domingo."

"Domingo," Clint said, "if I were to see you in the street facing three or more men, I would be inclined to step in and back your play."

"Señor," Vazquez said, spreading his hands, "that is all I have ever hoped for."

* * *

They left the cantina, Vazquez kissing his sister good night, Clint and Carmen bidding each other good night primly.

Clint and Vazquez walked away, heading back to the part of town where Clint's hotel and Cantina Carmelita were located.

"A drink in the cantina before you go to your hotel?" Vazquez asked.

"Why not?"

They entered the cantina, finding it crowded and noisy. Girls were working the floors, games were going on at the tables. The bar was crowded, but space opened up miraculously for the two of them. Clint was sure it had nothing to do with him.

"*Dos cervezas*," Vazquez told the bartender.

"*Sí, Jefe.*"

When they had their beers, Vazquez turned to Clint and raised his mug.

"To my sister, Carmen," he said.

"Carmen," Clint repeated, wondering where this was leading.

"She is a gem, señor," Vazquez said, "and should be treated as such."

"Agreed," Clint said.

"Please remember that," Vazquez said. "I would not like it if anyone was to hurt my sister." He'd implied this over supper, but now he was saying it outright.

"I understand, Domingo," Clint said.

"Excellent," Vazquez said, slapping Clint on the back. "Now we are truly amigos."

TWENTY-NINE

Hal Chance walked around town for several hours, never saw anyone matching the description they had been given. He ended up in front of the cathouse, decided to take a break and go inside.

The place was well stocked with Mexican girls and nothing else, which suited him just fine. He had planned on sampling as many Mex gals as he could while down here. So far, though, Rydell had kept him from doing that. But now, with Rydell not around, he was free to sample all the Mex gals he could.

"Señor?" an older lady asked. She wore a black dress and had a black comb in her hair, from which hung a black veil. "Come in, come in, señor. The girls are waiting."

She led Chance into a parlor, where black-haired, dark-skinned gals of all sizes and shapes sat.

He was in heaven.

Rydell put a fresh pot of coffee on the fire as darkness fell. He had the uncomfortable feeling that Chance was doing something stupid. But he hoped it was something like spending hours in a bordello, rather than finding their man and facing him alone.

But knowing his partner as he did, his money was on whores. Chance probably didn't have the gumption to face their man alone, but he was stupid enough to be spotted.

Just go to a whorehouse and fuck all night, he thought. It was the safest thing for both of them.

Clint finished his beer with Vazquez, turned down the offer of a second, and said, "I'm going back to my hotel. Thank you for the supper, Domingo."

"*Por nada*, señor," Vazquez said.

"I'll see you tomorrow."

Vazquez nodded, and as Clint went through the batwing doors, Vazquez signaled the bartender for another beer.

The door to the office opened and Ernesto Paz stepped out. Vazquez wondered if the man had been watching him and Clint Adams at the bar.

Paz came to the bar, and without being asked, the bartender put a glass of whiskey on the bar. Customers at the bar cleared out and gave the two men a wide berth.

"So?" Paz asked. "How was supper?"

"Very good," Vazquez said. "We went to see my sister."

"Ah, the lovely Carmen . . ." Paz said.

"Don't say it," Vazquez said warningly. He did not like that Paz was constantly trying to hire Carmen to work in his cantina.

"*Lo siento*," Paz said, raising his hands. "I am only interested in what you and Señor Adams talked about."

"He agreed to help me, if it comes to that," Vazquez said.

"Really?"

"Does that surprise you?"

"Well . . ."

"Because you sent your man, Santana, to try to provoke him?"

"And he did not."

"He did not wish to kill a man—or three men—over a chair," Vazquez said.

"Or he is not the man we think," Paz said, "and he was frightened."

"Trust me, he is not frightened."

"So you say," Paz said. "And I suppose, for your sake, we better hope not."

Paz drank his whiskey, turned, and walked back to his office.

THIRTY

Hal Chance put his hands behind his head and watched the Mex gal's head bob up and down in his lap as she gobbled his cock.

He had asked in the parlor for girls who would do this sort of thing. Not all whores provided what they called "French" services, and in Mexico, a lot of them had not even heard of such a thing. But this girl, Pilar, was not only willing, but anxious to do it for him. At least, that was how he saw it. In point of fact, Pilar was known by the other girls as someone who would do anything to anybody for money.

Pilar said, "Mmmmmm," as she sucked Chance's cock wetly, sliding one hand beneath his balls to fondle them at the same time. As he erupted into her mouth, he thought he had sure picked the right whore this time . . .

Pilar sat back on her heels on the bed and smiled at the gringo with the small *polla*. She knew he wouldn't last long, and she was right. As soon as she sucked him and touched his *cojones*, he was finished.

"How was that, señor?" she asked.

"That was amazin'!" he said breathlessly. "Are there any other girls here who would do that?"

"No, señor, just me."

"What about . . . you know . . . from the back?"

"The back, señor?"

"You know, putting my johnson in your . . . back hole? Any girls do that?"

"Ohhh," she said, giving him a sly look, "señor, you are a very bad man."

"Yeah, I am," Chance said, still trying to catch his breath after she had sucked him dry. "So, are there any of the girls that'll let me do that?"

She smiled, turned around, and shook her big, bare ass at him.

"What about me, señor?"

His eyes bugged out as she reached back and separated her ass cheeks, presenting him with her little pink anus.

"Oh my God!" he said, reaching for her, but she scampered away.

"Hey!"

"Señor," she said, shaking her index finger at him, "you must pay me for what we did, and then we will talk about what else we will do."

Chance grabbed for his pants, took out some money, and handed it to her.

"Okay, so now . . . how much?"

She smiled as she stood up, walked to her dresser, put the money in the top drawer, then walked back to him, making sure he got a real good look at her going and coming.

"Now, señor," she said, "exactly what do you want to do to me?"

"Well . . ."

After Paz walked away, Sheriff Vazquez started to wonder where the other gringo in town had gone. According to the hotel register, his name was Hal Chance. He'd never heard of the man, and still didn't find him on the wanted posters by name. If he wasn't in the cantina, looking for a girl or a game, what was he doing?

The only other place he thought he might be was the whorehouse. If he was, then he was no danger to anyone but those girls, and they had their own way of taking care of things there.

"Another one, *Jefe?*" the bartender asked.

"No," Vazquez said. "Have you seen Santana?"

"No, *Jefe.*"

"Tell him I am looking for him."

"I will, *Jefe.*"

Vazquez knew the bartender would "yes" him 'til he was blue in the face, and then do whatever Ernesto Paz told him to do.

"*Buenas noches, Jefe,*" the man said.

Vazquez turned and walked out.

When Clint got to his hotel room, he kicked off his boots, unbuttoned his shirt, and sat down on the bed. He ran through his conversation with Domingo Vazquez, wondering if the lawman had told him the truth the whole night. And if not, why lie? Of course, the one who could tell him if Vazquez was lying was Carmen—and that was if she would tell him the truth. And if she would even come to him tonight, considering her brother had seen them together.

He picked up the Alexandre Dumas novel from the table next to the bed, decided to read until either Carmen showed up or he started to fall asleep.

THIRTY-ONE

He was dozing when there was a knock on the door. He roused himself, set the book aside, took his gun from the holster on the bedpost, and walked to the door.

"Who is it?"

"It's me," Carmen said. "Who were you expecting?"

Well, since the three men had tried to provoke him into a fight earlier, he couldn't be sure. He opened the door, still holding the gun ready, and saw Carmen in the hall, alone. He opened the door.

"You are being very careful, señor," she said, slipping in. "Is there something wrong?"

"Just some men showing an interest in me," he said. He walked to the holster and slid the gun home.

"Why did you and my brother come to the cantina today?" she asked, removing the shawl from her head.

"I didn't take him there," Clint said. "He took me."

"Did you tell him about us?"

"No," Clint said, "but I didn't know if you had."

"I do not tell my brother all about my life, Clint," she said, "and he does not tell me all about his."

"I see. Well, he sure made it sound like he knew about us," Clint told her.

"Why? What did he say?"

"Nothing obvious," Clint said. "Just some veiled threats about what he'd do to anyone who hurt his sister."

"Domingo plays the doting big brother when it suits him," she said.

"Well, I guess it's suiting him, then," Clint said.

"Did he frighten you?"

"No," Clint said.

"Did he ask you for help again?"

"Yes."

"Help with what?" She sat on the bed.

"He told me some men he arrested several years ago have escaped from prison and might be coming here."

"But why? Everyone in Mexico knows my brother and is afraid of him."

"Not these men, apparently," Clint said. "He said there were three of them, and they've recruited some other escapees."

Carmen looked concerned.

"If these men come for my brother, will you help him?" she asked.

"That depends."

"On what?"

He sat next to her on the bed.

"Carmen, is he telling me the truth? Did he send those men to prison years ago for bank robbery and murder?"

"My brother has sent many men to prison."

"For bank robbery? And murder? Here in town?"

"I—I was not here—I only came back to Laguna Niguel two years ago, Clint."

"Where were you?"

"Mexico City," she said. "I thought I could make a life there, but it did not happen."

"Why not?"

"Men," she said. "They wanted me to . . . to do things. To work for them. For money. Things that I would not do for money. Even here, Ernesto Paz constantly tries to get me to come to work for him."

"I'm sorry," Clint said. "I know what men can be like."

"But not you," she said. "Why is that?"

"I just see the world differently, I guess," he said. "I see women differently."

She leaned into him, put her head on his shoulder.

"Do you think we could sleep tonight?" she asked. "Just sleep, holding each other?"

"Sure, Carmen," he said. "We can do that."

But they sat that way for a while.

Later, while she was sleeping on his left shoulder, he listened intently for sounds outside the hotel, outside his room. He hated to think it, but what if Carmen was trying to keep him busy? After all, he'd only known her a short time. Had she been playing him all this time? Along with her brother? And if so, why? For Paz, the powerful man?

There were no sounds, no one sneaking down the hall to his door. Clint knew the smart thing for him to do was leave in the morning, head back to the border. But he had a friend here, Avery Castle, and his pregnant wife. He had to make sure they would be safe.

If Paz and Vazquez were up to something, why would Vazquez be asking him to stay?

He reached up with his right hand, touched his gun. His pistol and his horse, they were the only things he could truly trust.

In the morning he'd talk to Avery, and come to a decision whether to stay or go.

While Carmen slept soundly on his shoulder, he tossed and turned most of the night, until the morning sunlight streamed through the windows.

THIRTY-TWO

When Clint woke up in the morning, realizing he'd slept after all, he shook Carmen awake.

"Come on, honey," he said. "I've got to go. There are things I have to do."

"What about breakfast?" she asked as he ushered her out of the room.

"I'll be eating with a friend."

Clint washed with the pitcher and basin in the room, dressed, and left his room. He walked to the beach, made his way to Avery Castle's house.

Meanwhile, another stranger rode into town, missing Clint by moments. Cord Rydell rode down the street, keeping his eyes peeled, and reined in when he came to the livery.

"*Buenos días, señor*," the hostler said.

"Like to put up my horse."

"For how long, señor?"

"A day or two. How many hotels you got in this town?"

"Two."

"Okay." Rydell took his saddlebags and rifle and left the stable.

Where the hell was Chance?

*   *   *

Hal Chance woke up in his hotel bed, his legs weak from the time he'd spent with the whore, Pilar. That gal had let him do anything he wanted, as long as he paid for it, and that was all right with him.

But the light coming in the window told him it was morning, and he hadn't found out a thing. Rydell was going to be upset with him. He had to get out there and find out where their guy was. But first maybe some breakfast . . .

Clint mounted the stairs to Avery's deck, found his friend sitting at the table.

"Lita!" Avery shouted. "We have a guest for breakfast!"

"*Bueno!*" she shouted back. "I will bring the coffee."

"I'm here for more than coffee, Avery," Clint said.

"I figured that," the older man said. "What's up?"

"You know a man named Santana?"

"Yeah," Avery said, "local muscle for hire."

"Somebody sent him and a couple of friends after me yesterday."

"What happened?"

"Nothing," Clint said, sitting. "I diffused the situation, but they sure looked disappointed."

"He does a lot of work for Paz."

"I figured that."

Lita came out with a pot and two mugs, poured coffee for them, and then hurried back to the kitchen.

Clint told Avery about his conversation with Sheriff Vazquez.

"You've been here five years. Was there such a robbery here a few years back?"

"I've been in Mexico five years, Clint," he said. "Not here exactly. I did hear something about a bank robbery several years back, while I was building this house, but I don't know the details. You think he's lying to you?"

"I don't know," Clint said. "Maybe I'm being set up, or maybe I'm just overly suspicious."

"Well, I say leave town," Avery said. "Leave Mexico. Get out before something happens."

"But what about you and Lita?"

"What about us?"

"Vazquez says he thinks there's more to you than meets the eye," Clint said. "What if I leave and he turns his attention to you?"

"If he does, I'll handle it."

"When was the last time you used a gun?"

"Doesn't matter," Avery said. "It's not something you forget. You know that."

"Yeah, I know, but—"

"Breakfast," Lita announced, coming out with a tray of steaming plates. "It is wonderful to have you here again, Clint."

"I think I'm becoming a pain in the ass," Clint said.

"Not at all," she said. "Avery has no friends here. I am happy you are here for him." She surprised him by kissing him on the forehead before returning to the kitchen.

"She's quite a woman," he said to Avery.

"Yeah, she is."

"No way I can leave the two of you here without knowing you're safe," Clint said.

"So what are you gonna do?"

"I'm going to have to make a statement."

"How?"

Clint shrugged, picked up a tortilla that was filled with eggs and steak.

"Maybe," he said before taking a bite, "it's time for me to go to confession."

•

THIRTY-THREE

As Clint approached the church, he saw Father Flynn outside, in the clothes of a peasant, on his knees at the base of one of the church walls. When he saw Clint approaching, he stood up, brushing the dirt off his hands by rubbing them together.

"You look like one of the locals," Clint said.

"Jesus was a plain man."

"Right," Clint said. "A . . . carpenter?"

"That's right."

There were other men working on different sections of the wall.

"Can we talk? In private?"

"Keep working," Father Flynn called out. "I will be back."

"Sí, Padre," one of them said.

"Come inside," Father Flynn said. "I have some lemonade."

"No more whiskey?"

"I have to save it," the priest said. "I might not have the money to buy any more."

"Maybe," Clint said, "I can make a donation."

"That would be most welcome."

Clint followed Father Flynn into the church, down the

side aisle to the front, and into the sacristy. They then walked beyond it, and into what he assumed was the priest's office. On the desk was a pitcher of lemonade and several glasses. Father Flynn poured two and handed one to Clint. It was ice cold in his hand.

"What's on your mind?"

"I'm thinking I may need someone to back my play."

Father Flynn stopped with his glass halfway to his mouth.

"And you decided to ask a priest?"

"I'm asking the man I used to know."

"The man you used to know is dead, Adams," Flynn said. "I can't help you."

"Don't even want to hear what the play is?" Clint asked.

"It doesn't matter," Flynn said. He drank some lemonade, then just stood there and looked at Clint.

"Tell me that if I search this room, I won't find your gun," Clint said.

Flynn didn't answer. Clint knew he was right. Flynn's gun and holster were somewhere in the room.

"Why would you keep it unless you thought you might have to use it again someday?"

"It would have to be an extreme case," Flynn said, "to get me to even consider it."

"I think I'm being set up for something, Father."

"Then get out while you can," the priest said. "If you know it's going to happen and you don't get out, then you're a fool."

"Well, color me a fool, then," Clint said, "because I can't leave. There are other people to consider."

"There always are with you," Flynn said.

"Do you know Avery Castle?"

"I've heard of him."

"He has a house on the beach," Clint said. "I would think you'd have seen him around."

"He's not one of my flock," Flynn said, "and I don't spend much time at the beach."

"He has a pregnant wife."

"And they are two of the people who may also be involved?" Flynn asked.

"Yes."

"Is your main problem with Sheriff Vazquez?"

"It is."

Flynn shook his head. "He has a big reputation in Mexico."

"So I've heard."

Flynn put his glass down. "I've got to get back to work."

"Vazquez told me he locked up some bank robbers and murderers a few years ago, and now they've escaped from jail and may be on the way here."

"So?"

"I'm trying to figure out whether or not he's telling me the truth."

"He's made a lot of arrests."

"Was there such a robbery a few years back?" Clint asked him.

"I wasn't here then."

"Some of your parishioners would probably know," Clint said. "Could you ask around for me?"

"I can do that much," Flynn said, "since you warned me of the sheriff's interest in me."

"I'd appreciate it."

Father Flynn walked Clint outside, where some of his flock were still working on the wall.

"If I get any answers," Flynn said, "I'll send them along to your hotel with a messenger."

"Thanks . . . Father."

Clint walked away, then turned and watched as Father Flynn joined the members of his flock kneeling at the base of the church wall.

He assumed that a threat to the welfare of his church would qualify as an extreme case.

THIRTY-FOUR

Rydell saw Chance's name in the hotel register, which confirmed how stupid he was, signing his own name. Rydell signed in as Tom Brown. "John Smith" would have been just too obvious.

He dropped his gear in his room, then walked down the hall to Chance's room and knocked on the door. There was no answer.

He went down to the front desk.

"Have you seen Mr. Chance today?"

"Chance?" the clerk asked, frowning.

"The gringo who rode in yesterday."

"Ah, room six," the clerk said. "Yes, I saw him early today, señor, going out just before you arrived. Is he a friend of yours?"

"No, no," Rydell said, "don't even know him. I just saw another gringo name in the register and thought I'd say hello."

"Well, he did ask me for directions to a, uh, certain house in town," the man said.

"Ah," Rydell said, "I understand. And where would that house be . . ."

*   *   *

Chance was walking around town, but again he didn't see
anyone matching the description they had. There were, however, two places he hadn't looked yet. One was the church,
and the other was the beach, where, apparently, some people
actually had houses. He didn't understand living near the
water like that, but then he'd never even seen the ocean.
Might as well take a look now, though . . .

Clint walked back to town, wondering what he should do
next. He'd talked with both Avery and Father Flynn, pretty
much the only people in town he would be honest with. He
knew who they were, and they knew who he was. There was
really nothing to hide.

    As he was approaching his hotel, he saw the same three
men who had approached him the day before about the chair.
One of them was sitting in it. Apparently, they were going
to try him again. He wasn't feeling as charitable as he had
been the day before. Maybe dispatching this trio would keep
anyone else from bothering him.

    He continued on to the front of the hotel.

Rydell was walking down the street, heading for the cathouse to look for Chance, when he saw three men facing
one in front of the town's second hotel. He stopped to watch,
with interest.

As Clint approached the hotel, the seated man—the spokes-
man from last time—remained seated as the other two
turned to face him.

    "Sorry, amigo," the seated man said, "today the chair is
mine."

    "Don't mention it," Clint said. "Today I'm not interested
in sitting."

    "Are you interested in going into the hotel?" the man
asked.

"That's what I'm aiming to do."

One of the other men put his foot up on a post, effectively blocking Clint's entry through the front door.

"*Lo siento*, señor," he said, obviously *not* sorry.

"Move your leg, friend," Clint said.

"Did you hear the gringo, Armando?" the seated man asked. "He told you to move your leg."

Armando looked at Clint with a grin and said, "No spikka da English."

All three men laughed until Clint grabbed the man's leg and pulled him off the boardwalk, dropping him unceremoniously onto his butt in the street.

The man glared up at Clint with fury in his eyes, and his hand started for his gun.

"Go ahead and do it," Clint said. Then he pointed to the standing man. "You put your hand near your gun and I'll kill you first."

Hastily, the man moved his hand as far away from his gun as he could without detaching his arm.

Clint looked down at the man on the ground.

"You want to use that? Then stand up," he said. "Otherwise just stay where you are."

The man thought it over, then his shoulders slumped and he remained on the ground.

For the first time Clint turned his full attention to the man in the chair.

"What's your name?"

"I am Santana, señor."

"You want to take a shot, Santana?"

"No, señor," the man said. "I am just sitting here."

Clint walked past all three men carefully and entered the hotel lobby. From there he watched the one man get up from the ground, and then all three men cross the street and walk away—though how far he didn't know.

"Señor," the desk clerk said.

"Yes?"

"That was Santana, señor."

"I know," Clint said. "He introduced himself."

"He is *muy malo*, señor. Very bad man."

"I'm hearing that about more and more men in town," Clint said. "Is there anyone in this town who isn't *muy malo*? First Sheriff Vazquez, then Santana. What about Ernesto Paz?"

"Sí, señor," the clerk said. "Señor Paz is very bad."

"And these very bad men, do they ever face each other?" Clint asked.

"That would be silly, señor."

"Why's that?"

"Well, because they are all connected."

"In what way?"

"Simple," the clerk said with a shrug. "They work for Señor Paz."

"I thought Vazquez worked for the town."

"Oh no, sir," the clerk said. "Señor Paz named Señor Vazquez as the sheriff."

"There was no election?"

"No, señor."

That was very interesting.

"What happened to the previous sheriff?"

"Well . . ." The clerk seemed reluctant to answer that question.

"Come on, now," Clint said. "After everything you've told me, you're not going to keep that back, are you?"

"I suppose not, señor."

"Then what did happen to the former sheriff?"

The clerk shrugged and said, "Señor Vazquez killed him."

"How?"

"Out there, in the street," the clerk said. "He is, uh—"

"*Muy malo?*"

"Sí, señor," the clerk said, "and very deadly with *la pistola*."

"So I've heard. Now I've got another question."

"Sí, señor?"

"Why are you telling me all this?"

"Because, señor," the clerk said, "you are the Gunsmith, are you not?"

"I am."

"Then señor," the clerk said, "you are also *muy malo*, are you not?"

"Yeah," Clint said, "yeah, I guess I am."

THIRTY-FIVE

From across the street, Rydell watched the action, and watched as the three Mexicans walked away, defeated by the gringo.

He thought he knew who the gringo was, but he wanted to make sure.

He crossed the street and peered in the hotel window. The gringo was talking to the desk clerk. He watched and waited. Eventually the gringo nodded, walked away, and mounted the stairs, presumably going to his room.

Rydell entered the hotel and went to the desk.

"Señor, may I help you?" the clerk asked. "Do you need a room?"

"I have a room, thanks, in the other hotel."

"Oh, señor," the clerk said, "our rooms are so much better."

"I'm sure they are, but I'm fine. All I need is a bed," Rydell said.

"We have better beds."

"I saw a man come in here, and I think he was a friend of mine," Rydell said, ignoring the man's sales pitch.

"Señor?"

"A tall man, just now," Rydell said.

"Ah, you mean Señor Adams."

"Yes, that's him. Clint Adams, right?"

"Sí, señor," the clerk said. "He is *muy malo*. A very bad man."

"That's what I've heard," Rydell said. "Thanks."

"Do you want his room number?"

"No, that's okay," Rydell said. "I'll surprise him when I come down."

He turned to leave, then stopped and turned back.

"Don't tell him I was askin'," Rydell said. "I want to surprise him, okay?"

"Of course, señor."

Rydell nodded and left the hotel. As he came out, he spotted a man hurrying down the street, and went to meet him.

After scouting the beach and the church, Hal Chance came running back to town. He had to find Rydell and tell him what he'd found.

When he got to the main street, he saw Rydell come out of the town's second hotel. He rushed to intercept him.

"Cord!"

"Not here!" Rydell said, going past him. "Meet me at the cantina."

"But which one?"

"The smallest one," Rydell said, and continued on.

Rydell found the smallest cantina in town. It served drinks, but no food, no girls, and no gambling. For that reason, it also had practically no business.

Perfect.

He ordered a beer and settled down to wait.

Chance checked two cantinas before he found the right one. Rydell was standing at the bar. He went and stood next to him, ordered a beer from the bartender. They waited for the bartender to walk away before they spoke.

"I found him!" Chance said.

"Did you?"

"Yeah."

"When?"

"Today. This morning."

"Was he alone?"

"No, he had somebody with him."

"Did he see you?"

"No."

"Are you sure?"

"Dead sure."

"You better be."

"So what do we do?"

"You're gonna take me and show me," Rydell said. "When I'm sure, then we'll move."

"Okay." Chance started away from the bar but Rydell stopped him.

"Not now! Finish your beer. Relax," he ordered. "This has to look natural."

"Okay," Chance said, "I get it."

"What about the local law?"

"Supposed to be a really hard man," Chance said.

"Have you met him?"

Chance hesitated.

"Aw, Chance . . ." Rydell said.

"I couldn't help it," Chance said. "I was having a drink in the big cantina and he walked up to me."

"Did you make eye contact?"

"Just once, when I had to."

"Does he suspect you?"

"He's a lawman," Chance said, "I'm a stranger. I'm sure he suspects me. But there's no paper on me, remember?"

"I remember."

"Guess you better avoid him, huh?"

They both knew there was paper out on Rydell in both Texas and Arizona.

"I will."

They finished their beers.

"Okay, you go out first. Wait for me at the end of the street, in a doorway or alley or something."

"Right."

Hal Chance pushed away his empty beer mug and left the cantina.

"Another, señor?" the bartender asked.

"No," Rydell said. "What do I owe you?"

Rydell paid what he owed and left the cantina. He found Chance waiting in a doorway.

"Okay," he said, "show me."

"This way."

They left the doorway and Chance led the way.

THIRTY-SIX

Clint went to his room and moved directly to his window, which overlooked the front of the hotel. He looked for the three Mexicans but didn't see them. He did, however, see two other men, who looked like gringos.

They didn't seem to know each other, but one of them looked like he had come out of the hotel. They walked past each other without seeming to acknowledge one another, which was odd for two gringos in a Mexican town. When you came across a countryman in a foreign country, you tended to talk, if not bond. These two had ignored each other.

Or had they?

He left the room and hurried down to the lobby. The clerk looked up quickly as he approached.

"Was anybody in here looking for me?"

The clerk hesitated, and stammered.

"Well . . . he told me not to tell."

"It's okay," Clint said. "You can tell me. What did he want?"

"He just said you were friends, and he wanted to surprise you."

"How nice. Thanks."

"Did I do anything wrong, señor?" the clerk asked nervously.

"No," Clint said, "nothing at all."

He left the hotel.

He looked both ways on the street, did not see anyone. Not the Mexicans, not the gringos. Only some of the town citizens, and not many of them.

Clint headed for the sheriff's office.

As he entered the office, Domingo Vazquez looked up from his desk.

"Clint."

"Domingo," he said, "do you know anything about two gringos being in town?"

"You mean other than you?"

"Naturally."

"Just one other," Vazquez said. "A sloppy-looking gringo at that."

"Well, I saw a sloppy-looking one, but I also saw another one."

"Were they together?"

"They took great pains not to seem to be together," Clint said.

Vazquez frowned.

"This is not your trouble, is it?" Clint asked. "Were any of the escaped prisoners gringos?"

"No, they were not," Vazquez said. "Perhaps these two are here for you."

"Speaking of somebody being here for me, I had another run-in with those three Mexicans."

"Yes?"

"I dissuaded them again."

"Any bloodshed?"

"None."

"Well, that's good." Vazquez stood up, took his sombrero

from a peg on the wall. "I suppose I should look into these two gringos."

They walked outside together.

"What will you be doing?" he asked.

"Not sure," Clint said. "Maybe I'll go and have a talk with somebody who might be able to shed some light on everything."

"Will you tell me who that would be?" Sheriff Vazquez asked.

"I will," Clint said, "as soon as I figure it out."

They split up.

THIRTY-SEVEN

Clint went to the Cantina Carmelita. He knew who he wanted to talk to, he just didn't want to tell Vazquez. He didn't want the lawman around for the conversation.

It seemed all the *muy malo* men in town worked for Ernesto Paz, so it was Paz he decided to talk to.

He stopped at the bar and ordered a beer.

"Is Señor Paz in?" he asked when the bartender brought the beer.

"Sí, señor."

"Would you tell him I'd like to see him, please?" Clint said. "My name is Clint Adams."

"Of course, señor," the bartender said. "I know who you are."

The bartender left the bar and walked to the back of the room. The thing about the Carmelita was that it was so big it was always doing a good business, no matter what time it was. Clint looked around at the bored faces in the place. He didn't see any of the three Mexicans he'd encountered twice in front of his hotel, or either of the two gringos he'd seen in the street earlier.

The bartender returned and said, "*Por favor*, this way, please, señor."

"Gracias."

He followed the bartender to the door in the back, where the man said, "You may go in, señor."

"Thanks."

Clint had been in many saloon offices in the United States. This one was hardly any different, with a desk, some chairs, some files, and Ernesto Paz sitting behind the desk.

There were many experiences Clint had repeated over and over again in his life. This was one of them.

"Ah, Mr. Adams," Paz said. "Please, have a seat."

Clint sat across from Paz.

"Some brandy?"

"No, thanks," Clint said. "I'm fine."

"What can I do for you?"

"You can call your men off," Clint said. "I don't know what your goal was in sending them to harass me, but it has to stop. There may be some real trouble headed this way, and I can't be wasting my time with them."

"Well, I am disturbed to hear that trouble is coming," Paz said, "but I don't understand what you are saying about my men. What men?"

"One of them is named Santana," Clint said.

"How do you know his name?" Paz asked.

"He introduced himself."

Ernesto Paz looked annoyed that the man had volunteered his name.

"You know Santana, don't you?"

He saw Ernesto very briefly consider lying, before he spoke.

"Sí, he works for me."

"So why would he come after me himself?" Clint asked. "You sent him, didn't you?"

"I did not," Paz lied. "Perhaps he wanted to test his mettle against the famous gringo, the Gunsmith."

"Well, if that was it, he didn't do a very good job of it," Clint said. "Look, whether you sent him or not, he works for you. So you tell him I don't have time for him. If he braces me again, I'll kill him. Got it?"

"I have it, señor," Paz said. "I will pass your words on to Santana."

Clint stood up.

"If I have to kill him, or one of his compadres, I'll hold you responsible, and I'll be back to see you."

Paz stiffened. So far all that Clint had seen in the man was an amiable attitude. Suddenly he was cold.

"I do not take well to threats, señor."

"Then don't consider it a threat, Señor Paz," Clint said. "Consider it a promise."

Clint did not wait for the man to say anything in return. He'd made his point, and he walked out.

THIRTY-EIGHT

Rydell and Chance approached the church.

"There he is," Chance said.

"Where?"

"There," Chance said, pointing.

"I see a bunch of peasants, most of them old men, and a priest."

"Right."

Cord Rydell looked at Chance and said, "What the hell, Hal?"

"Look at the priest, Cord," Chance said. "That's him."

"I gotta get a closer look."

They walked up to the church together. The people stopped working to look at them. The priest turned and stared at the two of them.

"Jesus Christ," Rydell said. "It is you."

"I don't know—"

"Don't deny it," Rydell said. "Just go inside and get your gun."

"I can't do that," Father Flynn said.

"Why not?"

"I'm a priest."

"That's crap."

"No," Father Flynn said, "I really am a priest."

Rydell stared at him.

"This is a dodge."

"No, it isn't," Father Flynn said, "I have been ordained."

"I don't care," Rydell said. "I ain't sayin' you ain't a priest. I'm sayin' you became a priest as a dodge."

"What do you want?"

"I've been hired to kill you," Rydell said. "You left behind some people who hate you."

"I'm sorry about that."

"That won't do," Rydell said.

"Then draw your weapons and kill me," Father Flynn said, spreading his arms.

"We will," Rydell said, "but I'm tellin' you to go inside and put on your gun."

"I don't have a gun."

"That's crap, too," Rydell said. "Even if I retired, I'd keep my gun. You have, too."

"I can't put a gun on again."

"I tell you what," Rydell said. "If you don't put on your gun, we're gonna kill you anyway—but first I'll kill all of them." He pointed at the men who had been working on the church.

"You can't."

"I will!"

From behind the church a man named Enrique heard all of this. The two gringo gunmen had not seen him, so he turned and ran to town.

Clint was coming out of the Carmelita when he saw a man running down the street.

"Señor, señor," he said breathlessly.

"Take it easy," Clint said. "What's wrong?"

"Señor, I saw you at the church," the man said. "You are friends with Father Flynn?"

"I am," Clint said, rather than explain his real relationship with the priest.

"They are going to kill him, señor."

"Who? Who's going to kill him?"

"Two gringo gunmen," he said.

"What's your name?"

"Enrique, señor."

"Enrique, go and tell the sheriff what you told me."

"Señor, you will not let them kill the priest?"

"I'm sure going to try," Clint said. "Now go!"

Enrique ran toward the sheriff's office, while Clint took off running toward the church.

THIRTY-NINE

When Clint came within sight of the church, he stopped. The two gringos were outside, with a bunch of Father Flynn's parishioners. Father Flynn, however, was nowhere to be seen. Clint assumed the priest had been allowed to go inside the church to get his gun.

He circled around behind the church so he could enter from the back. Once inside he found his way to the priest's sacristy, and then his office, where he found Father Flynn sitting at his desk with his head in his hands.

"Father."

Flynn looked up with an anguished look on his face.

"I can't," he said. "I can't kill . . . but if I don't, they will kill my people."

"So I heard."

"Wha—how did you—"

"A man named Enrique came and got me."

"I wondered where he was," Flynn said. "I thought he was hiding."

"I sent him to get the sheriff."

"He probably won't get here in time."

"All right, look . . . Father. I'll go out there for you."

Father Flynn lifted his face from his hands and stared at Clint.

"I will . . . but you're going to owe me a favor."

"A favor," Flynn said. "What kind of favor?"

"I'll tell you when the time comes."

Flynn was about to say something else when a voice came from outside.

"Time's up, Father," the man shouted. "I'm gonna shoot the first one."

"All right, all right!" Flynn said. "I owe you a favor. Anything! Just don't let them shoot any of my people."

"All right," Clint said. "Stay here."

He turned and walked to the front of the church.

"What if he don't come out?" Chance asked Rydell.

"He'll come out," Rydell said. "He ain't gonna let us kill any of these people. Not if he's really a priest."

"Yeah, but what if he don't care? What if he went out the back door and he's gone?"

A look came into Rydell's eye, but it disappeared when a man stepped out of the church.

"That ain't the priest," Chance said.

"No," Rydell said, recognizing the man from in front of the hotel, "it ain't."

Clint stepped out, saw the two men right away, standing with some of Father Flynn's parishioners.

"Okay, you can let them go now," he said.

"Oh yeah? Why's that, friend?"

"Father Flynn isn't coming out," Clint answered. "You get me instead."

"How's that?"

"Father Flynn is a priest," Clint said. "He can't strap on a gun."

"We're not here for Father Flynn," Rydell said. "We're here for the man he used to be."

"Well, that man's dead," Clint said. "Instead, you get me."

"Who is this fella?" Chance asked. "You ever see him before, Cord?"

"Yeah," Cord said, "I saw him in front of the hotel. He faced down three Mexicans."

"That a fact? Kill any of 'em?"

"No, just dumped one in the dirt and then invited them all to go for their guns."

"And none of them did?"

"Nope."

"So who is he?"

"I don't know," Rydell said, "and I don't care. We gotta go through him to get to the priest."

"We can do that," Chance said.

"Yeah, we can."

"No," Clint said, stepping away from the doorway, "you can't."

"Move," Rydell said to the peasants, waving them away.

They ran off, but not so far that they couldn't watch.

Rydell moved away from the church, as did Chance. Clint could see these two had done this before. They made sure there was a lot of space between them.

"You're makin' a big mistake, mister," Rydell said. "This ain't your affair."

"I'm making it my affair."

"But why?"

"I've got to go to confession," Clint said. "Can't do that with a dead priest, can I?"

"Mister," Rydell said, "I'll let the priest live just long enough to give you the last rites. How's that?"

"Stop talking," Clint said.

The two men went for their guns.

Clint didn't know their names, never did learn them. Rydell was slightly faster; Clint could see that as they both reached for their iron. So he drew and shot Rydell first, through the chest. He knew it was a killing shot without even checking. He immediately turned his attention to the other man—Chance—and shot him in the stomach before he could clear leather.

Chance's eyes went wide as the bullet punched him. All the air went out of his lungs. He never did get the gun out. He went down onto his butt in a seated position, a frown on his face. He looked down at his belly, which was leaking blood, tried to cover it with both hands, but instead his hands dropped to his sides, and he fell over sideways, face in the dirt.

Clint walked over to them and checked. They were both dead.

"Señor," Enrique said, running up to him. "You did it."

Clint looked at him, looked around for Vazquez.

"Where's the sheriff?"

"I could not find him, señor."

"All right," Clint said. "Go inside and get Father Flynn."

"Sí, señor."

As Enrique entered the church, Clint ejected the two spent shells, reloaded the gun, and holstered it. The other men came back toward him slowly, unsure of what to do.

"You fellas can go back to work," he said.

They stared at him.

"Uh . . . *trabajo*," he said, "back to work!"

Suddenly, they understood, and went back to what they had been doing.

FORTY

Father Flynn came out of the church, followed closely by Enrique.

"You killed them," he said.

"They didn't leave me much choice."

Father Flynn walked to the bodies and knelt down.

"What are you doing?"

"They deserve the last rites."

"They were going to kill you."

Father Flynn looked back over his shoulder at Clint.

"They still deserve the last rites."

Clint shook his head as the priest began to pray over the two dead gunmen.

Sheriff Vazquez showed up several minutes later, after Father Flynn had finished his prayers.

"*Que pasa?*" he said. "What happened here?"

"These men tried to rob the church," Clint said.

Vazquez looked at him.

"And you stopped them?"

"I just happened to be here."

Enrique was off to the side, speaking to the other men, who had once again stopped working when the sheriff approached.

Vazquez approached them and spoke to them in Spanish. Several of them answered his questions, and then he turned to look at Clint and Father Flynn, who were standing side by side.

"They support your story, señor," he said.

"That's because it's the truth."

"Sí," Vazquez said. He looked down at the dead men. "Do you know who they were?"

"The two gringos I told you about."

"Their names?"

"I don't know."

"Well," Vazquez said, "I will track them down, see if they registered at one of the hotels. And I will have some men pick up the bodies."

"Thank you," Father Flynn said. "I've already given them the last rites."

Father Flynn walked over to his parishioners, spoke to them through Enrique. Vazquez walked over to Clint and stood next to him.

"Fair fight?" he asked.

"It was very fair," Clint said. "I let them draw first, didn't I?"

Vazquez nodded.

"Maybe this was the trouble you were expecting," Clint said.

"I do not think they escaped from prison," Vazquez said. "I think they came here looking for someone."

"Then why would they try to rob the church?" Clint asked.

"I don't know, señor," Vazquez said, "and I cannot ask them."

The sheriff walked away, back toward town.

Father Flynn came over and stood next to Clint as the men went back to work.

"You lied to him."

"And your people backed my play," Clint said. "They're loyal to you."

"They're loyal to the church."

"Not the church," Clint said. "The man."

"Maybe."

Clint looked down at the two dead men, one lying faceup, the other facedown.

"You know these two fellas?"

Father Flynn looked at the two men.

"Never saw them."

"But they were here for you, right?" Clint asked. "Specifically here for you?"

"Yes."

"What are you going to do?"

"About what?"

"Well, somebody knows you're here," Clint said, "and they know who you really are. They've already sent two men after you."

"All true."

"Then they'll probably send someone else eventually, once they don't hear back from these two."

"Probably."

"You're just going to stay here and wait?"

"This is my church."

"But . . . what will you do when they get here?"

"Trust in God."

"God didn't save you today, Father," Clint said. "I did."

Father Flynn looked into Clint's eyes and said, "He sent you, didn't he?"

Clint looked back at him.

"Remember," he said. "You owe me a favor."

"Don't worry," Father Flynn said, "I'll remember."

Clint waited until the priest went back into the church, then walked toward town.

FORTY-ONE

As Clint walked back to town, he was passed by a buckboard with three men on it, one of them a deputy. They were on their way to pick up the bodies. It was not the deputy Clint had met, but he exchanged nods with him anyway.

Clint wanted a drink, but he didn't want it at the Carmelita. He stopped into a smaller cantina, and ordered a beer from the bartender.

"What was that shooting, señor?" the man asked.

"What shooting?" Clint asked, and the bartender went away.

Clint nursed his beer, thought about the events of the past half hour. He'd been curious about the two gringos, knew they were together, but he was feeling gratified to know that they weren't there for him. They were gunmen for hire, but they hadn't been there for him. After the events of the past half a year or so, that was refreshing.

But then, he had still ended up killing two men, whether they were there for him or not. That didn't exactly leave him a happy man.

He finished his beer and left the cantina.

*   *   *

Sheriff Vazquez checked both hotels, and got the names of the two gringos. From there he went to the Carmelita to talk to Paz. When he entered, he saw Santana standing at the bar with two other men.

"Santana!"

The man turned, gave the lawman an insolent look.

"I sent word that I wanted to see you," Vazquez said.

"I do not work for you, *Jefe*," Santana said. "I work for Señor Paz."

Santana was a competent man with a gun. Some in town thought he would like to test Vazquez, but Ernesto Paz kept them apart.

"Well, stay away from Clint Adams while he is in town."

"I will if Señor Paz tells me so," Santana said, "not you, *Jefe*." He said "*Jefe*" with heavy sarcasm.

"Santana," Vazquez said, "you will push me too far one day."

"Perhaps," Santana said, "we both look forward to that day." He turned his back on the lawman.

Vazquez was tempted to smash Santana's face in, but instead he walked to the back, to Paz's office. He entered without knocking. Paz looked up from his desk in surprise.

"You must tell Santana to stay away from Adams," he said.

"I was just testing the man."

"You do not need to test him," Vazquez said. "He just shot down two gringo gunmen in a fair fight."

"Where did this happen?"

"The church."

"The church? Why there?"

"He and the priest say the two men tried to rob the church."

"Why would two gringos come here to rob the church?" Paz asked.

"Exactly," Vazquez said.

"Ah, you do not think it is true."

"There has always been something suspicious about that priest," Vazquez said.

"What was Adams doing there?"

"He said he just happened to be there."

"You don't believe that."

"Not at all."

Paz rubbed his jaw and said, "The priest, eh? What is his name?"

"Father Flynn," Vazquez said, "but that is probably not his name."

"Perhaps," Paz said, "the bishop can shed some light on this. I will send a telegram to Mexico City."

"Meanwhile," Vazquez said, "call Santana off Adams, or I will have to kill him."

"Send him in here on your way out," Paz said, "and I will talk to him."

"Fine."

Vazquez left the office and walked toward the bar.

As he passed Santana at the bar, he said, "Your boss wants to see you."

Santana turned and asked, "Don't you mean our boss . . . *Jefe?*"

Vazquez walked out.

Santana left his half-filled beer mug on the bar and went to Paz's office.

"You wanted to see me?"

"Yes," Paz said. "What do you think your chance would be against Vazquez?"

"Very good, señor. Why?"

"He might have the wrong idea about how big he is," Paz said. "I might have to deal with him."

"Which means I will have to deal with him, eh?"

"Just be ready, Santana," Paz said.

"*Sí, Jefe.*"

There was no sarcasm in the word "*Jefe*" at all.

FORTY-TWO

Clint got an idea on the way back to town. He stopped at the office of the local newspaper, the *Laguna Niguel Dispatch*. He asked the editor for stories about bank robberies in the last few years. With the editor translating for him, he found what he was looking for.

He left there and went to the telegraph office.

Vazquez was in his office when the telegraph operator came in.

"*Jefe*," the man said, "a telegram for you."

"Then give it to me!" Vazquez said, reaching out.

The clerk came forward and handed it to him.

"Go!" Vazquez said.

After the man left, Vazquez read the telegram.

Clint walked to the beach, waved at Avery, who, as usual, was on the deck. He climbed up.

"I'll tell Lita to make coffee," Avery said. "She's inside, knitting something for the baby."

"No, I'm fine," Clint said. "I just came to talk."

"About what?"

"I killed two men today."

"Wait!" Avery said. He went inside, came out with a bottle of whiskey and two glasses. He poured two drinks, handed Clint one. "All right, go."

Clint told him about the two gunmen who'd come from the United States looking for "Father Flynn."

"He wouldn't fight?" Avery asked.

"No."

"What would he have done if you hadn't come along?"

"Trusted in God, I guess."

"Then he'd be dead."

"Vazquez had the bodies removed."

"What'd you tell him?"

"That they tried to rob the church."

"He's not gonna believe that."

"No."

"What else do you have?"

"I checked with the local newspaper," Clint said. "I should've done it a long time ago."

"The robbery?"

Clint nodded.

"Bank robbery, and murder, just as Vazquez said. Two years ago."

"So Vazquez was tellin' you the truth. He does need your help."

"He was telling me the truth as far as it goes," Clint said. "There was a robbery, he did arrest the culprits, and he did send them to prison."

"And did they escape?"

Clint took a telegram from his pocket and waved it.

"I sent a telegram to the prison and got an answer right back. They had a break, and eight prisoners escaped. Among them were the three who robbed the bank here and killed three people. What nobody knows is how many of the other prisoners they've joined with, and whether or not they're really on the way here."

"What do you think?"

"I think if Vazquez sent me to prison and I got out, I'd head right here."

"So it's just a coincidence that the other two came here after the priest."

"As much as I hate coincidences, I'd have to say yes."

"What do you plan to do now?"

"I don't know," Clint said. "I'm still not sure I'm not being set up for something. I don't like Ernesto Paz, and Vazquez is connected to him, if he doesn't actually work for him."

"Then I say you should get out," Avery said, "and get out now."

"Yeah, you're right," Clint said. "I should."

"But you're not, are you?"

"No."

"I hope it's not because of your concern for us," Avery said.

"I just have to find out what's going on, Avery," Clint said. "I can't leave here wondering what it was all about."

"Then ask somebody," Avery said. "Sometimes the only way to get the answers you're lookin' for is to ask."

"Yeah, you're right," Clint said. "And I guess the person to ask is Vazquez."

"You want me to come with you?" Avery asked.

"Still got your gun?"

"I got it."

"Lita would kill me if I made you strap it back on, Avery," Clint said. "I can do this on my own."

"Just know that I'm here, if you need me. And I guessing Father Flynn now knows he owes you a favor."

"I let him know."

"Good," Avery said.

Clint stood up and shook hands with his friend, climbed down from the deck, and walked back to town.

FORTY-THREE

Clint stopped at the sheriff's office, was told by Deputy Benitez that Vazquez was at the undertaker's.

As he entered the undertaker's office, a man of medium height dressed in a black suit was talking with a woman in widow's weeds and her family.

"I will be with you in a moment, señor," he said.

"I'm looking for Sheriff Vazquez."

"He is in the back, through that curtain."

"Gracias."

Clint went through the curtain, where he found two tables with the men he'd killed laid out. Off to the side Vazquez was going through their clothes.

"Sheriff."

Vazquez looked up and appeared surprised to be Clint standing there.

"What brings you here?" he asked. "Looking for information on the two men you killed?"

"I don't care about them," Clint said. "I want to talk to you about Jaime Garcia and his men."

Vazquez dropped the clothes he was holding and turned to face Clint.

"What do you know about Garcia?"

"Nothing," Clint said. "That's what I want to talk to you about. If you're really worried about them coming here—"

Vazquez held up his index finger to cut Clint off.

"I never said I was worried about Jaime and his men," Vazquez said. "I'm concerned for my town that they may come back for revenge. I want to be able to protect the town. I know I can protect myself."

Clint studied the man, trying to decide if he was telling the truth or not. It made a difference if the man was asking him to help the town, and not to help him personally.

"What's the word you have on these men?" Clint asked.

"I received word that they're on their way here," Vazquez said, "probably a day away."

"That close, huh?"

Vazquez nodded.

"How many?" Clint asked.

"Jaime, his two men," Vazquez said, "and three of the other escaped prisoners."

"What about Federales?" Clint asked. "I mean, these men did escape from a prison."

"I have sent telegrams to Mexico City," Vazquez said. "The Federales and I do not have a good relationship. I think they would be happy to hear that I was killed, and then they would come in."

"They might just ride in here and find a town burned to the ground."

"Exactly what I am thinking."

"All right," Clint said. "I need to know something before I decide to throw in with you."

"And what is that?"

"What's going on with you and Ernesto Paz?" Clint asked. "And why the hell is he pushing me with this Santana?"

"Paz and I have a relationship," Vazquez said. "But he does not own me. As for Santana, very soon I will kill him myself. Paz is worried about Garcia and his men coming to town, and when you appeared here, he decided that you might be the town's salvation."

"And how did you feel?"

"I am the law," he said, "so I am the town's salvation—but I would like your help."

"And what about Santana? Why's he pushing me?"

"Paz decided to test you," Vazquez said, "to see if you are still the Gunsmith. He was disappointed when you did not kill Santana."

"And you?"

"I was glad," Vazquez said. "I told you, I want to kill Santana myself."

"What about when Garcia comes to town? Can you count on Santana for help?"

"We can count on Santana to run and hide until it is all over."

"Okay," Clint said, "okay."

"What does this mean, 'okay'?" Vazquez asked.

"It means I'm with you," Clint said. "I'll help you be the savior of the town when Garcia comes with his gang."

Vazquez walked to Clint and shook his hand.

"I must make a confession," he said.

"What's that?"

"When you arrived, I was very tempted to try myself against the Gunsmith."

"Is that right? And now?"

"I no longer feel the need."

"That's good. I also have something to say, though."

"What is that?"

"Avery Castle," Clint said. "I want you to leave him and his wife alone."

"And the priest?"

"Yeah, him, too."

"Who are they really?"

"That's what I mean," Clint said. "It doesn't matter who they used to be, it only matters who they are now. I need you to agree with me."

Vazquez shook Clint's hand again and said, "*Bueno*, I agree."

FORTY-FOUR

It took three more days of waiting before Jaime Garcia arrived with his men.

Sheriff Vazquez posted his deputies so they'd be able to see riders from pretty far off. He had them spelling each other so that they were on watch for almost twenty-four hours a day.

On day three, Deputy Soto came running into the sheriff's office and said, "They're coming, Sheriff."

"How far out?"

"Less than an hour."

"How many?"

"I am not sure. There is a lot of dust."

"All right," Vazquez said, standing up from his desk and strapping on his gun. "Go to the hotel and tell Clint Adams. He will be sitting out front."

"*Sí, Jefe.*"

"And then I want you and Benitez off the streets."

"But Jefe—"

"No argument, Manuel!"

"*Sí, Jefe.*"
Soto left to run to the hotel.

Clint met Sheriff Vazquez at the north end of town.
"How far?" Clint asked.
"Half an hour."
"How do you want to play this?"
"Head on," Vazquez said. "I want to try to scare them right away."
"It's your call."
Clint looked at the dust in the distance. They looked closer than half an hour to him. Turned out he was right. They rode into sight twenty minutes later.

Jaime Garcia reined his horse in. The men behind him did the same. Arturo Montoya rode up alongside him.
"Is that him?" he asked.
"That is him," Garcia said. "Vazquez."
"Who is that with him?"
"Probably some fool deputy."
"So only two of them," Montoya said. "You said he would not get much help. You were right."
"*Sí.*"
"What shall we do?" Montoya asked.
"I know Vazquez," Garcia said. "He thinks he is saving the town. Either he will kill us, or we will kill him and be satisfied with that."
"But we will not be satisfied, will we?"
"No," Garcia said, "we will kill him, and then burn the town down anyway."
"*Bien,*" Montoya said. "That suits me."
Garcia waved and urged his horse forward.

"Here they come," Clint said.
"*Coño!*" Vazquez swore.

"What is it?"

"I see . . . eight of them."

"That's more than you figured."

"Yes."

"Change of plans?"

"Too late."

"Maybe not," a voice said.

They turned and looked, saw Avery Castle striding toward them, wearing a gun.

"Señor Castle."

"Sheriff."

"Avery."

"Couldn't let you do this alone, Clint."

"Can't argue with you right now, Avery," Clint said, "but if you get killed, Lita's going to kill me."

"Then don't let me get killed."

"We'll do our best."

"Still eight against three," Vazquez said.

"Lousy odds," Clint said.

"Maybe I can improve them," another voice said.

They all turned, saw the priest, Father Flynn, walking toward them with a gun strapped on over his coat. He was still wearing his collar.

"You said I owed you a favor," Flynn said to Clint.

Clint knew what he was doing. He had no intention of drawing that gun. He hoped some of the men would refuse to fight against a priest.

"Okay," Clint said, "now the odds are two to one. Slightly better."

As Garcia and his men approached, one of them called out, "Is that a priest?"

"Looks like one," Garcia said.

The man who spoke was named Vaca. He rode up alongside Garcia.

"You did not say we would have to fight a priest."

"I didn't know anything about it," Garcia said. "He's probably not even a priest."

"I do not care," Vaca said. "I will not shoot at a man in a collar."

He turned his horse and rode off, and one other man rode with him.

Now there were six.

Vazquez and his compadres saw that two of Garcia's men had ridden off.

"That collar worked, Father," Clint said.

"I hoped it would," Father Flynn said with relief.

"You can go, Father," Vazquez said, "with my thanks."

"Are you sure?"

"Yes."

"*Vaya con Dios*," Father Flynn said, and walked back to town.

"Vazquez!" Garcia called out.

"Garcia."

"Where is your priest?"

"He served his purpose."

"Sí, he did. He chased two of my men away."

"Maybe the rest of you should have followed them."

"Who is this?" Garcia asked. "I do not see a deputy's badge."

"This is my amigo, Clint Adams."

All six men stiffened, and one of them said, "*Hijo de un cabrón*, the Gunsmith?"

The men looked at each other, and then one of them said to Garcia, "We did not expect to have to fight the Gunsmith."

Frustrated, Garcia snapped, "Go, then!"

And two of them did, wheeling their horses and riding off at a gallop.

And then there were four.

"And this man?" Garcia said.

"A friend of mine," Clint said, "but we won't be needing him." He looked at Vazquez, who nodded.

"Señor Castle, you can go," Vazquez said.

"Are you sure?" Avery asked.

"Go, Avery," Clint said. "Give Lita a big kiss for me."

"Good luck, boys," Avery said, and walked away.

Now it was four against two—still two-to-one odds, but Clint had dealt with that before.

"Who do we have?" Clint asked.

"Garcia, his two men, and one other escaped prisoner I know nothing about."

"What about Garcia and his two?"

"Competent gunmen."

"Okay."

"Just stay to your side," Vazquez said, "and I'll stay to mine."

Garcia and his three men dismounted, and spread out. Their horses trotted off. As it turned out, Garcia was on Vazquez's side. Clint hoped the lawman was as good as everyone said he was.

"I thought about this for two years in my cell, Vazquez," Garcia said.

"Stop talking," Clint said.

"*Bastardo!*" Garcia said, and went for his gun. His men followed.

As Vazquez had said, they were competent gunmen. Not fast, but they drew and fired coolly, without panic. Their kind killed a lot of men—usually.

Clint drew and fired several times, just to be sure. His two men both spun as they were hit. They jerked their triggers, but they were shots fired into the ground and air with a death jerk of the trigger finger.

Vazquez drew. He knew Garcia was the better of the two,

so he keyed on him. He fired twice, as Garcia fired once. Vazquez felt pain in his left shoulder, but ignored it until he had shot the second men.

The four escaped prisoners were dead.

Clint and Vazquez checked the bodies. Avery and Father Flynn had not gone far. They came walking over, having watched the action.

"You all right?" Clint asked Vazquez, indicating his shoulder.

"There is no bullet there," Vazquez said. "It kissed me and continued on. I am fine."

They bent, made sure the men were dead, then straightened.

"What about the other four?" Clint asked.

"I could form a posse and go after them," Vazquez said, "but that is a job for the Federales. I will send a telegram and tell them where to find them."

"Do you mind if I give them the last rites?" Father Flynn asked.

"Go ahead, Padre."

Father Flynn knelt by the men and prayed.

"What are you gonna do now, Clint?" Avery asked.

"I'll be leaving tomorrow," Clint said.

"Tomorrow?" Vazquez asked.

"That's right. You disappointed?" Clint asked.

Vazquez turned and faced Clint.

"Or have you changed your mind about trying me?"

Vazquez narrowed his eyes. Avery and Father Flynn watched the two men. There was a hint of tension in the air. If it thickened any more, the two men would go for their guns. Each man thought he knew who would come out on top.

"Domingo?" Clint said.

Vazquez studied Clint a little longer, then put out his hand.

"I have not changed my mind, señor," the lawman said.

"And I appreciate your help." He looked at Avery and Father Flynn. "All of you."

Clint shook the man's hand with relief. He would have hated to kill Domingo Vazquez.

Watch for

MAGIC MAN

388th novel in the exciting GUNSMITH series
from Jove

Coming in April!

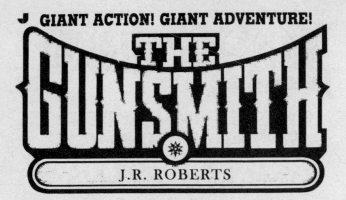

GIANT ACTION! GIANT ADVENTURE!

THE GUNSMITH

J.R. ROBERTS

LONGARM

GIANT-SIZED ADVENTURE FROM
AVENGING ANGEL LONGARM.

BY TABOR EVANS

penguin.com/actionwesterns

M456AS0812

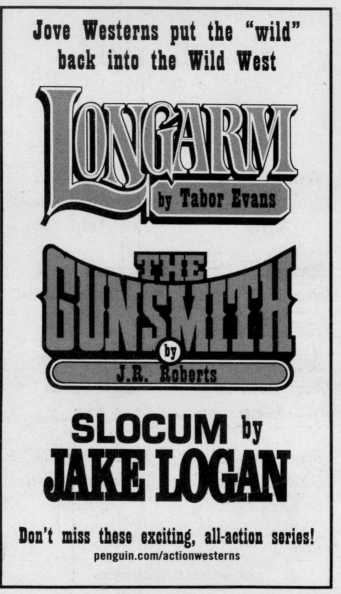